LEFT ALIVE

GRACIELA LIMÓN

Arte Público Press
Houston, Texas

This volume is funded in part by grants from the City of Houston through the Cultural Arts Council of Houston/Harris County.

Recovering the past, creating the future

Arte Público Press
University of Houston
452 Cullen Performance Hall
Houston, Texas 77204-2004

Cover illustration and design by James Brisson
Cover illustration by Alejandro Romero

Limón, Graciela.
    Left Alive / Graciela Limón.
        p.   cm.
    ISBN-10: 1-55885-460-6 (pbk. : alk. paper)
    ISBN-13: 978-1-55885-460-4 (pbk. : alk. paper)
    1. Psychiatric hospital patients—Fiction. 2. Children—Crimes against—Fiction. 3. Murder victims' families—Fiction. 4. Death row inmates—Fiction. 5. Women journalists—Fiction. 6. Women murderers—Fiction. 7. Mass murder—Fiction. 8. Infanticide—Fiction 9. California—Fiction.   I. Title.
    PS3562.I464L44   2005
    813¢.54—dc22   2005045261
                                                                    CIP

♾ The paper used in this publication meets the requirements of the American National Standard for Information Sciences—Permanence of Paper for Printed Library Materials, ANSI Z39.48-1984.

5 6 7 8 9 0 1 2 3 4   10 9 8 7 6 5 4 3 2 1

ACKNOWLEDGMENTS

Left Alive has taken its present form thanks to the help of so many of my friends and colleagues. However, before recognizing these great friends, I should explain that there is an original version of the novel. That manuscript was read and critiqued by Peter Limón, Rae Lunetta, Mary Wilbur and Irene Melford Williams. Their views and ideas were enormously important in moving my work toward its final version. I'm hugely grateful to them.

Diana González LeMere and Irene Melford Williams, both life-long elementary school teachers, have provided not only expert input after reading the second manuscript, but more importantly they have shed light on the lead character's probable behavior during his early school years. I cannot say how grateful I am for their ideas and responses.

Dr. Ricardo Machón, my colleague, friend and professor of psychology at Loyola Marymount University, has carefully viewed my character's deviant behavior and given me invaluable advice. Marlene Leiva Bermúdez, attorney and friend, has also read the manuscript giving me keen insights into those aspects of the novel that touch upon the character's obsession with his mother's trial and conviction. I sincerely thank you both for sharing your expertise.

I could not end this acknowledgement without thanking Gabriela Baeza Ventura and Nicolás Kanellos for their careful and diligent editing. These skilled editors have read both versions of *Left Alive* and guided me every step of the way. Your patience is boundless. I'm also deeply grateful to those of the APP staff who have worked to produce this novel: Marina Tristán, Mónica Parle, Linda Garza and Alejandro Romero who has created the outstanding cover artwork. To every one of you, *muchas gracias!*

DISCLAIMER

Children who survive a mother's murderous rampage have inspired *Left Alive*. The story line and characters are fictitious. Any similarity to people and places is coincidental.

G.L.

I shall kill my children.
No one shall take them from me.

What point is there in living?
Oh, oh, I want to end my hateful life,
Leave it behind and die.

Medea
(Euripides)

She weeps when the sun is murky red;
She wails when the moon is old;
She cries for her babies, still and dead.

She seeks her children day and night,
Wandering, lost and cold;
She weeps and moans in the dark and light,
A tortured, restless soul.

La Llorona
(A Mexican Legend)

*To Marlene Leiva
whose assistance and support
made this novel possible*

CHAPTER 1

Absalom House Sanitarium, 2002.

Elena Santos, a reporter for *The Register,* was nervous because she had never been in a mental hospital. She sat waiting for her name to be called, feeling stiff and somehow threatened although there was no reason for her apprehension. She was waiting not to be pushed into a ward but to interview one of the patients. His name was Rafael Cota.

She shifted her weight, trying to ease the pressure around her waistband. She had put on a few pounds recently but she knew that she would get rid of that little bit of bloat just as soon as she got back to working out. A few sessions of cycling or running would do it. In the meantime, she sucked in her paunch and slid her fingers under her jacket to rearrange the roll of flab that was causing her discomfort.

Elena refocused on her surroundings. Time seemed to drag so she tried to distract herself by taking in the details of the waiting room, but the antiseptic feeling of the place stunted any curiosity or interest. Gray enameled walls. Gray metal chairs. Gray linoleum. The glow shed by the overhead neon lights bathed the olive tones of her complexion with a greenish tint.

She waited empty-handed except for her purse and a battered briefcase where she had stashed newspaper clippings, Internet printouts, and other notes she had gathered on the case. Elena glanced at her wristwatch whenever she sensed a long chunk of time had passed, but each time she looked she discovered that she was wrong; only a few minutes had passed.

She threw a quick look toward the entrance thinking that it would be easy to walk out of the room, but she knew she would not do that because the path leading to this place had been long and hard for her. It had taken a ton of research about the man she was about to meet. Getting the necessary go-ahead to be admitted to where she was sitting had also been a huge challenge. It had taken months of wrangling with the hospital staff and, after that, plenty of waiting. No, she would not leave. Instead she again shifted her rump on the metal seat, for once feeling grateful for her hefty behind; it gave extra padding against the cold, hard surface.

"Miss! It'll be a while before Mr. Cota will be available."

A white-uniformed nurse interrupted Elena's musings. He seemed to have appeared from nowhere and vanished just as swiftly.

"Thanks!"

She reached for the briefcase and placed it on the chair next to her. Thinking that it would be a good time to dig through the stuff, she opened the case and pulled pages at random. *Only surviving child of mass murderer mother now in mental hospital.* This headline was the bait that had hooked Elena into searching out more information on the case, so now she gazed at the clipping for a long while, rereading parts of it. *Salinas, California. November, 1979. Three sleeping children murdered by a mother gone berserk.*

Next she pulled out a faded article from the bottom of the pile. *King City Strawberry Festival.* It was a three-column piece she had written for *The Register;* it was dated a couple of years before. She shoved it into a side pocket wondering how it had gotten mixed in with what she had collected regarding the Cota murders.

Elena sat back, arms folded over her stomach as she mentally traced her steps leading to this moment. She had held a reporter's job for the small independent newspaper for about three years, covering one event or another and, although what she wrote was mostly gossip, she was pretty good at it. She followed through on stories and was usually successful because she zeroed in on the human side of whatever it was that she was reporting. Her desk had been nicknamed the Big Ear by the staff because most phone calls were funneled to that station, putting Elena smack-dab in the middle of Salinas chitchat and sometimes a little bit of scandal.

While she waited to be taken to Rafael Cota, she relaxed against the back of the chair thinking of all the people she had interviewed, all the miles she had driven from one town to the other, always in search of the Big One. She thought of the dusty roads leading to small places like Chowchilla, Madera, and King City, towns where folks did not even bother to lock their doors at night. And yet this peaceful, safe place is where the Cota murders occurred, leaving everyone stunned. Now, on the verge of facing the sole survivor, Elena was trying to explain how such a thing could happen in her part of the world.

The story had been brought to her attention by the editor in chief of the newspaper. She was not sure why one day he inexplicably plopped the article on her desk, but whatever his reasons, she felt immediately drawn to the story. Maybe it was because she had grown tired of covering the ordinary stuff, the festivals and the beauty contests. Her most exciting stories recently had covered a brawl that had broken out at the fair between a couple of ruffians, and the other one was about kids that had discovered unguarded tractors and raced them down a turnip field, nearly destroying the crop.

Elena understood that people wanted to read about everyday things, but she was losing interest in that type of reporting. She longed to find what she considered the real meat that made for serious journalism. She had kept these thoughts to herself but when that big headline hit her, she knew that here was that something that might satisfy the hungry feeling inside her.

She decided to look into the case, hoping to discover details and dates that might give clues to the crime committed by a mother, a deed that somehow was responsible for her son now cooped up here in Absalom House. Night after night, Elena returned to her desk during after hours to dig into the Internet for more information and articles describing the circumstances of the crime.

Elena uncovered most of the facts. More than twenty years before, Rosario Cota had gone on a jealous rampage and murdered three of her four children, two girls and a boy, but inexplicably spared the youngest. These details alone intrigued Elena, but there was more to the story: Rosario Cota, whose appeals had run out, was now awaiting execution in San Quentin.

Deeply moved by what she read, Elena sensed that she had found a new avenue for her reporting and she experienced a huge surge of interest. The case had everything: jealousy, murder, a survivor, lunacy, capital punishment, and, best of all, it had happened right in her own neighborhood, so to speak. She felt inspired as never before, so during the next weeks she checked out newspapers and magazines to see if follow-through reports had been filed but none appeared, encouraging her to jump into the pocket and run with the story. She envisioned herself looking up Rafael Cota to get the story in his own words. Those interviews might even be the beginning of a series of hard-hitting articles exposing the crime of infanticide and the tale of a lone survivor nearly losing his mind after living through the ordeal.

Elena thought about it for days before she approached her editor with the idea; she had to be confident that he would share her interest. She cornered him one day while he sipped a cup of coffee. By that time Elena had the project clearly mapped out in her mind so that when she described it she was able to put her plan into words. As she heard herself speaking she became even more enthused, but when she finished she saw that her boss was hardly moved. Hands wrapped around the cup, he nursed it without saying anything until he finally nodded—indifferently, she thought.

"What got you going on this piece?"

"You did. Don't you remember giving me the article?"

"Nope."

"Well, you did and I'm hooked."

"Okay, if you think it's worth your time to run after this old story, that's up to you. It's fine with me as long as you come up with your weekly column."

"I was hoping for a leave."

"What? Paid?"

"Yes."

"Well, Elena, let me think about it."

"Look! I know that what I'm about to produce will pay for the days off."

"You're not scared of getting near a nut?"

"No."

"I don't know."

"What's not to know?"

"It's an old story. Who's going to read it?"

"Are you kidding? A piece about a mom who snuffs her own kids in a fit of jealousy will hook anybody."

Elena's boss looked at her for a while as he considered her proposal, then he took a few slow sips of coffee. He was taking time making a decision, but after a while he scratched his head and forehead. He had made up his mind.

"Okay, you got it, but don't blame me if the whole thing goes belly-up."

In the beginning Elena had felt uneasy, but then she shook off her boss's frosty response, deciding not to let it diminish her determination. Right away, she began to dig and hunt with the intention of coming up with as much information as she could get from old files, newspapers, and court proceedings. She was even more energized when she got dates, names, and the trial transcript.

The biggest roadblock was getting clearance to interview Rafael Cota. When she applied she had to speak several times with the director who was reluctant in the beginning to grant her visitation permission. He explained that Rafael had been through a difficult time over the past year trying to cope with his mother's upcoming execution. He had even attempted to kill his father but had been released by the police after the elder Mr. Cota dropped charges. After that incident, an assault on unsuspecting customers in a restaurant had tipped the scales and caused Rafael to be committed to the high security asylum in Atascadero.

Elena would not be put off, however, and after long discussions the director acknowledged that now in the more relaxed environment of Absalom House, Rafael's mental condition had improved significantly over the past months. He had responded positively to medication, showing signs of recovery every day, and gone were the violent outbreaks except for sporadic mood swings. So considering all of this, Elena's petition was accepted.

Elena's mind now returned to the waiting room. She looked at her watch again realizing that even more time had passed without a sign of being taken to Rafael Cota. She slammed shut the lid of the briefcase, put it aside, and got to her feet, deciding to get a reason for the delay. Just as she approached the male attendant seated behind the glass partition, she heard someone calling her.

"Miss Santos, please follow me."

Elena quickly picked up her bag and briefcase. Still feeling jittery, she followed the white-uniformed nurse through a locked double door and down an austere corridor leading to an outdoor porch. He opened the screen door for Elena and pointed at a man seated in a wicker chair.

"Thank you."

"No problem. Take as long as you want, Miss."

Elena looked at the patient knowing that it was Rafael Cota, but because he seemed oblivious to her presence, she took time to observe him carefully. She was riveted by what she saw. He appeared young yet old. He had full dark hair, and his profile was chiseled and sharp. The skin on his face and hands was smooth; she could not make out a wrinkle, not even while standing just a few feet away from him. Everything she looked at told her that she was gazing at a young man, but soon she began to see that he was extremely thin and bony, his shoulders craggy and stooped. His legs were crossed at the knee, and he slumped into the chair much as an old man might crumple into his seat.

She felt shaken as she gazed at him, but she went on staring, taking in as many details as possible before he became aware of her. He was dressed in a long terry-cloth robe, and his feet were bare except for worn slippers. He sat very still, hardly moving, hardly breathing, and he was staring at the lawn that stretched out in front of him. He appeared lost in thought, as if trapped in another world. Suddenly he snapped his head in her direction; his move was so unexpected that she nearly dropped her bag and briefcase.

"So? Are we gonna stare at each other all day?"

Rafael's voice was harsh, and it intimidated Elena because she had not expected this threatening beginning. She knew that her coming was not a surprise since she had written to him in preparation for the interviews. But now she could see by the tone in his voice and the expression on his face that it was not going to be smooth. Again she thought of leaving the place; instead she pulled up a chair. Trying to hide her nervousness she decided to sit close to him, thinking that it might help break the ice.

"Good morning. I'm Elena Santos."

"I know."

A tense silence followed his words but, instead of letting her apprehension get out of hand, Elena took in a deep breath and decided to try another tactic. She knew it would not be easy.

"I'm ready."

"Ready for what?"

"Ready to do what I explained in my letter. I want to hear your story."

"No, you don't! What you wanna do is get all the shit on Rosario and how the fuck she whacked my brother and sisters."

The foul words slammed into her but she rolled with the feeling, reminding herself that bad language was probably the easiest part of his story. However, she did stare at him wondering if she had been clear about her intentions when she wrote to him. Maybe she had laid out her plans to the director and even the hospital panel, but somehow failed to reach Rafael. On the other hand, she had been warned of the unpredictability of his behavior, especially his unexpected mood changes. Maybe this was part of the way he always behaved.

After her mind scanned the steps she had taken before coming to see him, she knew without a doubt that she had indeed been as frank and detailed as possible with him and the thought struck her that he was putting her through some kind of test. She unbuttoned the top of her jacket because she needed a bit more air around her throat, then she forced her voice to sound as calm as possible.

"No. It's your story I want to hear. Nothing else."

"But you ask all the questions, right?"

"Rafael, that's usually the way an interview goes."

"Call me Mister Cota."

"Excuse me! *Mister* Cota! I'll be as clear as I can. My intention is to write about women who murder their children, but more importantly, I want to follow through on children who might have survived that ordeal. Your story might be the first of the series. I say *might* because if you wish I can forget about the whole thing, walk through that door, and leave you to dream about whatever it was you were dreaming a few minutes ago."

"Hey! What're you gettin' all fucked about?"

"Hey, yourself! And watch your words!"

Elena clamped her mouth shut because she felt her anger rising and she did not want that irritation to slip out. She was startled by her bluntness and even her defensiveness, but she saw that her response seemed to have cut through something in Rafael because his expression changed. She was beginning to understand that her encounter with him would be rocky and that she had to be prepared for the unexpected. He uncrossed his legs as he waved a hand in her direction.

"What kinda stuff do you wanna know?"

"Anything about you. Your childhood. School days. Friends. Jobs. Everything. Whatever you can remember. You're about twenty-four, aren't you? That's a lot of years to talk about."

Rafael chewed on his fingernails. It was obvious that he was weighing her words and perhaps even planning a strategy, but then he shifted in the chair so that she no longer could watch his eyes, only his profile. She got the impression that he had decided not to speak.

"Look, Mister Cota, let's do it another way. For openers, why don't you ask the questions? I'll try to answer as best I can."

He turned and glared at her for a long while. His eyes had narrowed with suspicion, but he at least seemed to be considering Elena's proposal. He crossed and uncrossed his legs, then stretched them forward, flexing his feet back and forth as if exercising them.

"Okay. What comes first?"

"I'd like to hear you tell me of your first recollections. You were a baby when it happened, so it's important to know when you began to take things in after that."

"*It. Things.* You can use the word *murder.* I'm used to it. Remember, I grew up hearin' all about how Rosario snuffed out the kids."

Embarrassed, Elena shifted in her chair. She decided to be blunt from that point on so she nodded, letting him know that she got the point, she waited for his next question.

"Well? What else do you wanna know?"

"My next question would be about your feelings, your thoughts. I'd like to know if you were afraid or felt lost."

"That's stupid. How do you think I felt? How'd you feel if you grew up all fucked up?"

"Fine! We can skip that. Instead, I might ask if you ever dreamed or made believe?"

"A fuckin' little Mickey Mouse, eh?"

Exasperated by his sarcasm and bad language, Elena slumped back into the chair not caring that she was glaring at him. Almost convinced that she was not going to get anything of value from him, she looked at her things, planning to leave.

"Okay, okay. What else?"

"I'd like to know about people who were important to you."

"Yeah! Go on!"

"I'm going to ask you what you experienced when you first met your mother."

Elena had already sensed that this might be a delicate subject with him, and she was right. She saw that these words jarred Rafael because his head jerked backward as if he had been punched. He closed his eyes, and his mouth strained into a straight, angry line and when he opened his eyes he frowned. This convinced her that she had touched something inside of him so she braced herself for a nasty comeback, but after a few moments she was instead surprised by his calm voice.

"Where're you from?"

"Southern California. The San Fernando Valley."

"No shit! That's far away. What're you doin' all the way up here?"

"I work for a newspaper near here."

"Where in the Valley did you live?"

"Van Nuys."

"That ain't good enough. I wanna know where in Van Nuys. Gimme a street."

"Our house is on Costello Street."

"A rich house?"

"No. It's a regular place."

"Any brothers or sisters?"

"Yes, I'm one of three girls and two boys."

"Hey! Them's a lotta kids. Was you spoiled?"

"Not more than most kids."

Elena kept her eyes on Rafael as he crouched deeper into the high-backed chair, understanding that he had turned the conversation around; now the focus was on her. She decided to go along with his questions and waited for whatever was coming next. After a few minutes he looked straight at her.

"How old are you?"

"I just turned thirty-four."

"Are you married?"

Now she felt a surge of defensiveness push aside her willingness to answer. The thought hit her that Rafael was moving into the privacy of her life. She knew, however, that if she retreated at this point, she might as well walk away.

"No, I'm not married."

"Why not?"

"I've never been asked."

"Why not? What's wrong with you?"

"Does not being married mean there's something wrong with a person?"

"Hey! No questions! Remember I'm the one in charge. Okay. I'm gonna try again. What's wrong with you?"

"Nothing is wrong with me!"

Elena's voice was getting raspy, loaded with outrage. She wanted to slap his face and decided that she would do just that if his next question were as impertinent. She held her breath when she saw that he was getting ready to spout out something else.

"So, where do you get it?"

"Get what?"

"You know what."

"No, I don't!"

"Fuckin'."

"Shut up!"

"What?"

"I said shut your big mouth!"

Elena grabbed her bag and briefcase as she got to her feet so abruptly that she nearly knocked over her chair. She wanted to slug him but instead she charged toward the door. Her heart was pounding with rage, and she felt her face burning with humiliation. All she wanted was to reach her car to escape, but Rafael also jumped to his feet and he followed, reaching her before she disappeared into the building.

"Hey! Take it easy! I didn't mean nothin'. It was a big joke. Enough, already! Come on back so we can start talkin'. Now it's your turn. You can ask all the questions you want."

Rafael put his hand on Elena's arm, holding on so firmly that she felt its pressure through the sleeve of her jacket. She tried to yank her arm away, but his grip was like a vise. She looked down at it, then up into his eyes, and she saw that he seemed afraid that she would leave him. In that heated moment, she thought that she detected a plea in his eyes; it was sincere, intense, and it changed her mind. She relaxed her body and allowed him to lead her back to the chair, where he took her things and carefully placed them on the floor next to her. Then he quietly returned to his seat.

They did not speak for a while. Both were wrestling with the shock of their clash. Both were trying to find a way back to the beginning. For her part, Elena struggled to put aside her anger so that she might experience sympathy for the lost young man seated so close to her. She desired to understand him. She wanted to share the pain of being the child of a murderous mother. Perhaps this would show her the way to explain how such abuse could be survived. Maybe it would give meaning to whatever she wrote.

Elena took a deep breath knowing that what she was seeking would take a long time, that it would take more than one, two, or maybe even dozens of similar encounters. She braced herself for a long haul. For the time being, however, she felt drained, exhausted.

"I'm tired. I'll return tomorrow."

"Are you puttin' me on?"

"Do you want me to come back?"

"I'm a real asshole. Don't pay me no attention."

Elena stood and gathered her things, amazed at the transformation that had come over him. Then she looked out on the grounds seeing that it soon would be dark; the separation between lawn, trees, and night sky was blurring. It was time for her to leave. Rafael got to his feet unsteadily and made a faint gesture as if reaching out to get her hands, but he only lowered his arms.

"I'll be here after your breakfast. In the meantime think of what you want me to know about you and I'll be thinking of you."

"Yeah. I'll wait for you."

CHAPTER 2

Next day a nurse led Elena outdoors where she waited for Rafael to emerge from the building. It was an early December day typical of Central California, mild but with a touch of rain in the air. She settled into the high-backed garden chair; trying to calm her feelings, she breathed in the fragrance of grass and flowers. She had spent most of the night sleepless, thinking of the clash with Rafael the day before. Her resentment had deepened during those night hours, weighing heavily in favor of cutting off any encounters with him. He had embarrassed her, and she had not been able to lash back, not as she really would have wanted; she had to admit that he frightened her.

On the other hand, Rafael had a story to tell and this alone attracted her, compelling her to put aside hurt feelings or anything else that might come afterward. She weighed these thoughts carefully and before she finally fell into a deep sleep she decided that she would not allow Rafael's manner to interfere with the project. His was a story that had to be written; all she had to do was forget whatever bad behavior might come along and listen to what he had to tell.

Elena was deep in thought when she saw him. From her vantage point she watched Rafael walk toward her, this time dressed in white pants and shirt. She looked at him as he crossed the lawn. He was something like six feet tall, with too little weight for that height, but scrawniness did not affect the way he walked and swung his arms.

"Good morning, Mr. Cota."

"Call me Rafael."

She raised her eyebrows as she watched him retrieve a chair to sit facing her. After trying a few spots closest to her, he flopped into the chair, crossed his legs, and folded his hands on his lap.

"Gotta smoke on you?"

"No. I don't smoke."

"Don't you do nothin' bad?"

"I thought you promised that from now on I would ask the questions."

"Right! Okay! Let's hit it!"

Elena reached into her briefcase and pulled out a tape recorder. She checked the buttons to make sure the battery had juice and then she put it on her lap. Rafael, attracted by the machine, reached over and took hold of it.

"What's this bugger?"

"A recorder. I need your permission to record our words."

"Permission? From me?"

"Is it okay?"

"Yeah! Where do you wanna start?"

"Anywhere you want. It's your story that's important. Begin anywhere you want."

"This is tough. The only people I talk to are asshole shrinks, and they ain't like you."

"What do you mean?"

"They ask the same fuckin' questions all the time. It makes it easy for me to give 'em a loada bullshit."

"You lie?"

"Yeah. It's easy. I know what's comin' next so I always give 'em a crock and they swallow it."

"Rafael, do you want to talk to me?"

"Yeah."

"Then don't give me any nonsense because even though I'm not a shrink I'll be able to tell when you're putting me on. Just tell me what happened to bring you to this place. Tell me what you remember and why you've done all the things I've read about."

"Read about? I bet you ain't read that I tried to murder a sonofabitch."

"Your father? Yes, I've read that, and other things."

"And you ain't spooked?"

"Of what?"

"Me."

"No."

"Shit! You're one tough *mamacita*!"

"When are we going to get to your story?"

"Okay! Okay! But it's long."

"I'm ready."

"I wanna begin not when I was a kid but with a crazy dream that comes to me all the time."

"A dream? Why not leave that until later? It'll be a bigger help for me to get to know about you first, then you can tell about the dream."

"Hey! Yesterday you asked me if I dreamed. Now you changed your mind. What's up?"

Elena looked hard into Rafael's eyes, asking herself what difference would it make if the interview didn't go in the precise way that she had structured it in her mind. Maybe a dream had as much importance to him as what happened during his school days, or even during the years that had gone unaccounted in all she had read. Something told her that flexibility might be the best way to reach Rafael.

"Okay. Let's start wherever you want."

"What I see in that dream is the real thing each time it comes round. It's somethin' that's bugged me ever since I started to grow up. It keeps gettin' bigger till it runs me down like a giant steamroller, leaving me all fucked up.

"The things I see are weird, sometimes blurred, sometimes clear like I was on weed or some other junk. My mind takes me back to the house where the crap happened and even if I was too little to remember, I can see the place. I swear it! Believe me, it ain't the pills the shrinks gimme that puts them pictures in my brain. I go to the house in different ways. Sometimes I feel that I'm flyin' and that I swoop right into the place through a window or a door."

"Rafael, you were only a year old when your father took you away from that house. Could it be that what you think you dream is probably from descriptions you've heard, or maybe pictures you've seen in newspapers?"

"Maybe, but if I try real hard, I can hear my brother's and sisters' voices talkin' and laughin' in the kitchen. I even hear the clinkin' of forks on dishes and the ice in their soda glasses. I see everythin', like the walls still remember what happened when the kids lived inside 'em. That don't sound like I got all of that from stinking pictures or newspapers, does it?

"Then what I see gets real crappy. When I hear their voices I feel a big pull that wants to drag me away. I know that I'm feelin' chicken but I just can't help myself and I stay to hear more of the giggling and horsing around. But them happy sounds all of a sudden change into Rosario's and my old man's thick, mad voices. They scream at each other and start to throw things. He tells her that he's had it with her, that he don't like the way she is, the way she looks, the way she smells. Then she yells that she knows he's fuckin' around with bitches, that he's forgettin' that she's the main one in his life, that he's makin' fun of her and that she ain't never gonna let him get away with it. I hear this shit and get all messed up. Just then they stop yellin' and I hear the sound of glasses fill up with stuff from a pitcher. How can people just stop yellin' and start boozin'?"

Rafael abruptly stopped speaking so Elena looked at him not knowing what was coming next. She had been absorbed with his story and the interruption jolted her; it took a few seconds for her to realize that he was asking her a question. Without waiting for her response, however, he went on talking so rapidly that he was mumbling, words tripping on words.

"That happens all the time and after a few seconds they go at it again, gettin' nastier, meaner. The racket gets louder and I get real spooked 'cause I don't know what's gonna happen next. I hear my brother's voice tryin' to say somethin' but my old man chases him away, orders him to go to his room. My brother runs down the hall cryin' and yellin', then the girls run after him. Now Rosario and my old man are really pissed. Anyone can see that they hate each other's guts. Suddenly, he runs outta the house, slams the front door, and I hear him crank his car. He guns the motor real hard, then the noise drifts away and everything is quiet. Only Rosario's snivelin' fills the kitchen.

"I hear her fillin' another glass from the pitcher, then she turns off the light, walks down the hall, goes up to her room, and closes the door. I hear all this stuff. I swear it! Now I start to relax. I think it's all over. I sit wonderin' why nobody didn't even look for me, all alone in the crib like I was. Goddamnit! I ask myself why I don't cry my guts out with all that screamin' going on.

"This happens all the times my mind sneaks into the house. I just sit there in the crib without movin' and don't know jackshit about nothing. Everythin' is quiet 'cept I can hear the rain outside. Suddenly I hear the car again. The front door opens and slams; somebody runs up the stairs. Then the ugly voices start all over again. I hear a big racket, like people shovin' furniture around. There's grunting like somebody wrestlin', kickin' somethin'. I think I hear somebody scream out, *No! No!* Then a door opens and slams. A creepy quiet happens after this, like just before somethin's gonna fall.

"Then a big explosion shakes up the house. Right away I hear somebody runnin' to a room. Three more bangs. There's another scary quiet but nothin' happens. Then, oh, God! God! Somebody starts to howl and screech. It's a bummer, like a wild dog or somethin'. I can't tell if it's Rosario or my old man screamin'. There's more runnin'. I hear another blast. Then everythin's quiet. After a while I begin to smell somethin' that makes me wanna puke, smoke that stinks like shit."

Elena, riveted to the chair, watched as Rafael slumped back in his chair, sweaty beads glistening on his forehead and upper lip. She, too, was feeling a strange pressure on the pit of her stomach, but most of all she felt a growing concern for him. She reached over about to shut down the recorder.

"Are you sure you want to go on with this? We can talk about other things."

"Lemme finish tellin' it. After what I just told you happens, I creep outta the crib, slow at first, afterward a little faster."

"Rafael, you were a toddler, not walking yet."

"Hey! Don't interrupt me! It's a dream and anythin' can happen, right? I walk or maybe I crawl. It don't make no difference. What's important is that I make it outta the crib. Everythin' is quiet, nothin' is movin', but the lights are on everywhere in the hall, in the rooms. I make it first into the room where the girls sleep. They're in the same bed and there's blood smeared all over the place. It's splattered on the goddamn walls, on the covers, on their faces. Their heads are a big mess. Jesus!

"My heart is pumpin' so hard that it yanks against my chest, tryin' to run away. It wants to rip itself outta my body, outta that ugly place that stinks like shit. Then I run to my brother's room and there he is, eyes wide open, with a hole in his head. I run to him, shake him, scream at him. Get up! Get up! But he don't move, his big eyes bug out at me.

"By this time I can hardly breathe, the red shit stinks so much. It's gooey and smeared all over the place. Then I run to the room next door and there I am, just a little turd back in the crib, my fists openin' and shuttin'. This time my heart almost stops when I see what I looked like when I was small. I get real close and see that I'm awake."

"Rafael, I have to interrupt because you're losing me. Who is looking at whom? Are you a baby or a grown-up dreaming about being a baby?"

"How am I supposed to know? All that's for sure is that I put my arms around the little kid when suddenly I hear somethin'. I let go and look at the door where I see somebody movin', a shadow maybe, but I can't make out nobody. The dream stops right there. I don't see who pulled the trigger, all I know is that it wasn't Rosario."

Rafael, exhausted, stopped speaking, and Elena, moved by the gravity of his voice and the vivid recounting of his dream, nervously rubbed her forearms and hands. Nonetheless, she was unconvinced that it was a dream because what he had narrated came so close to published newspaper and police reports that it sounded like a re-telling of what he must have read or heard. On the other hand, she was awed by Rafael's stunning description of color, sounds, and smells; something not found in print. Most of all, she was intrigued by his certainty that someone other than his mother had committed the murders. She stared at him, puzzled and startled by the possibility of his mother's innocence, something that had not occurred to her.

"Rafael, when did you begin having this dream?"

"I don't remember."

"Are you sure you didn't read about it?"

"There you go again! I'm tellin' you that I remember it happenin' since before anythin' else, maybe even before I could talk. I know Rosario ain't guilty and this dream proves it."

"What about the physical evidence that came out in the trial? It proved her guilt. The jury was convinced."

"It was rigged, made to look like she did it. I know that the cops and lawyers lied. They're all a pack of goddamn liars, everybody 'cept Abuela. She always told me that Rosario was innocent and she put it in my head that it was up to me to prove it."

A picture flashed through Elena's mind: burly guards dragging Rosario to the execution chamber as she screams that she's innocent. That image, and the idea that the woman might be innocent, now gave Elena pause, but she quickly shrugged the thought aside because the proof brought to trial was too compelling, too damning.

"Tell me about your abuela."

"She was Rosario's mother."

"She told you to prove her innocence?"

"Yeah. That's why thinkin' this way ain't new for me. It's been with me ever since I first remember my dream and hung out with Abuela. All the time I been sure that Rosario ain't guilty, so when I growed up I went scroungin' around lookin' for people who remembered that night. I tried to dig up even a little bit of scoop that for sure could prove that I was right. I spent a long time lookin' for neighbors and even the maid who ran away to Mexico. I got gutsy enough to track down the cop in charge of the investigation and a nun who visited Rosario in the pen. I did all this tryin' to show that she didn't do it.

"But, do you know what? I came up dry and it drove me crazy. All that horseshit got so bad that it landed me here in the middle of a buncha nuts. I got all messed up, seein' things that ain't there, dreamin' weird dreams, hearing goddamned voices. When it was all finished, snoopin' around left me nothin' but empty hands and a fractured brain. Who cares? I'm still sure she's gonna get all pumped up with filthy chemicals for nothin'. She ain't guilty. That's all there's to it!"

When her conversation with Rafael ended, Elena returned to her car, walking slowly as if each step were bringing up new thoughts in her mind. She was reflecting on Rafael's deeply rooted conviction regarding his mother's innocence, a belief he now claimed his grandmother planted. Who could tell when she began to fill the boy's mind with those thoughts? Even Rafael could not trace when or how it began, but it seemed to Elena that the dream he described might not be a dream after all. Maybe his grandmother had been the first to tell him what happened in the house that night and he now thought of it as a dream.

Elena got into her car but did not turn on the ignition. Instead she sat staring through the windshield, still thinking of the role Rafael's grandmother played in his life. She was focusing on an adult's power over a child, in this case a grandmother who had perhaps inadvertently put that child on the road to Absalom House. This thought moved Elena to ask if that grandmother could have imagined the destruction that had overtaken Rafael because of his unmovable belief in his mother's innocence.

However, was this a fair question? Maybe, but maybe not, because why should that grandmother be blamed for defending her own daughter? What is so surprising about a mother believing in her daughter's innocence? No. What Rafael has done or not done, Elena told herself, is his responsibility, no one else's.

On the other hand, what if Rosario Cota were indeed innocent? Would this not vindicate both Rafael and his grandmother? This thought startled Elena. It was so completely off the mark of her mind-set that she pushed it away immediately. She shook her head, turned the key, and drove out of the parking lot. Tomorrow, she told herself, would be another day with new information to compile. The important thing for her was not to get caught in a rut over this idea, or any other one. What was important for the sake of her writing was to keep moving forward and not lose focus.

CHAPTER 3

Hours had passed but Rafael did not show signs of wanting to quit. Elena, however, was tired and ready to call it a day. She slumped back in the chair, a jumble of thoughts pressing in on her.

It's not possible that Rosario Cota is going to the gas chamber an innocent woman. What about the ton of evidence that's on record? What about the testimony telling of jealous possessiveness and obsessions? What about her claim of not remembering anything that happened that night? Granted, what was brought against her was circumstantial, but if she didn't commit the crime, who did? No! Forget it! There's no doubt. She did it.

The recorder had clicked off moments after Rafael stopped speaking, leaving only the chirping of birds and the distant hum of freeway traffic to fill the silence. After a while Elena suggested that they end the session when she saw that he had grown pale and drained.

"Let's break here. We can pick up tomorrow."

"No. Let's talk more."

She nodded, put a new tape in the recorder, reset it, clicked it on, and then signaled him to speak.

"I was left alive that night but for what? I'll tell you for what. I was left alive to live a life that's been a mess. It's been a stinkin' alley that's dead-ended me into this loony bin, leavin' me to fart around with a buncha basket cases. If you think that's being alive, then that's the story of my life.

"I'm the youngest of four kids, the one that got away when my brother and two sisters got whacked. You know what the record says. It says that Rosario Cota pulled the trigger on her kids. God! It pisses me to say it 'cause it ain't nothin' but a goddamn lie! Everyone says that it ain't possible for me to remember what happened. Those assholes say I was too little, but now I know they say it just to suck me into that big lie. I've always been scroungin' for answers, anythin' to help me prove that she's innocent. It was uphill and hard but I never stopped sniffin' around even when she blew me off."

"I thought you got to see her."

"Yeah, I finally got to be with her but before that I tried to see her. When I was just a kid. It was then that she turned me away."

"I don't understand."

"I asked to see her but she gave me the cold shoulder."

"She wouldn't see you?"

"That's right."

"Are you sure she refused to see you? Maybe there was a mix-up."

"Nope!"

"Maybe she couldn't get permission."

"Can't you understand what I'm sayin'? She just didn't wanna see me. It's simple. Any shithead can see that."

Moved by the edginess in his voice Elena backed away, more caught up by what he was saying, and she forgot her fatigue and her aching rump. Rafael was relating what she could not have found in transcripts or articles so she did not make a move to interrupt him, admitting that although she was feeling wiped out she wanted to hear more. Then he suddenly scooted to the edge of his chair, getting so close to her that she felt his breath graze her forehead and cheeks. He raised his hands, framing his face with his fingers as if it was a picture.

"Look at this mug. Tell me what you see. I'm twenty-four and I look like some ol' creep, don't I? Look at this bony, ugly face. It's brown and worn out, ain't it? I feel like I'm a hundred years ol' and my face shows it. I know that this is the honest-to-god truth when I look in the mirror. On my good days I try to talk myself into thinkin' that it's just worry that's got me lookin' this way, but it's no good givin' myself that pile of horseshit. I know it's the price I'm payin' for kickin' and scratchin' against the big lie. It's what hits you when your ol' lady is gonna be gassed even if she ain't guilty. What do you think of that? Can you imagine what it feels like? I wonder why I was born, why my ol' man didn't let up that one time so I wouldn't come around."

Rafael rocked back and forth on the chair as he spoke, and Elena, feeling a chill snake up and down her back, understood that he was not only telling the story of his life, but that his emotions were also spilling out, exposing his tormented insides. She felt afraid, not of him but of her inability to say something to lessen his pain. She decided to listen, thinking that talking might be the only way for him to recover the frayed thread of his life story. Maybe he would find a way back to some kind of peace.

"Hey! Lemme tell you what it's like livin' here with these basket cases. It ain't hard. It's quiet, unless one of the freaks torques off and screams or tries to climb the walls. When that happens the poor slob is put down fast with one quick jab of the killer needle to the arm. I swear, baby! That dope does the job. It's worked for me all kinds of times.

"When I'm not moppin' hallways or cleanin' johns I sit lookin' through the big windows makin' me think I'm free. But I know I'm not free 'cause when I look real hard I can make out a wire mesh that's built into the glass. Pretty smart, eh? But that's cool. I don't wanna break loose of this cage anyway. I'm so tired of roamin' and lookin'. I've had it with runnin' around tryin' to find the proof. At least now I can straighten out my brain and see what's got me here in the first place. Oh, yeah! I talk to myself most times, even when the faggot nurses gimme the evil eye when I get too loud, but I don't give a shit. Talkin' to myself helps me get through the long days and nights.

"Well, I guess I should get to the point, right? The story of the kids' murders is long, with lotsa twists and turns.

Lookin' back on the whole goddamn thing gets complicated. People tell it in different ways. There's the story Rosario stuck to in her trial when she tried to tell 'em that my ol' man drugged her and made her black out while someone else pulled the trigger on the kids. Nobody believed her. Then there's his big lie. After that, nobody can forget my aunts, uncles, Abuela, and even strangers and how they told their side, each time the whackin' got a new slant. In the end no matter who was blabbin', there was just one story: my brother and sisters was done in on that December night.

"Goddamn! My head feels like a toilet bowl with all the crap inside it goin' round. It hurts!"

"Rafael, let's take a break. I'm ready for it. Why don't we take some time and meet here in a couple of hours. Maybe you can rest a little."

"Okay."

Surprised that he so easily agreed with her, Elena watched him walk away toward the main building. He swayed, a little unsteady she thought. For her part, she welcomed the break because she, too, was feeling the beginnings of a headache. She got to her feet, arranged her things on the chair, and decided to take a walk to stretch her legs and back.

The December sky was beginning to pale but she found that the air was not chilly, so she walked under the oak trees. She took deep breaths as she moved, trying to overcome the shaky feeling that had taken hold of her stomach. Conflicting thoughts tumbled and clashed inside her because she was now uncertain as to how she would write Rafael's story. Its focus had shifted. It might not be a story of the child surviving a mother's murderous rampage after all. It might instead be the story of a woman unjustly condemned to die and how that cruelty had mangled her child's life.

Elena suddenly stopped walking. She thought that Rafael had implicated his father as the culprit. Was that the case? Maybe she was wrong in thinking she had understood that Rafael was accusing his father. Maybe she was getting everything all mixed up. Maybe her head was swirling just as much as Rafael's.

She returned to the chair thinking that she should quit the project; this story might be too big for her, even dangerous. She sat slouched back with her head tilted upward gazing at the sky. On the other hand, it might be too soon to quit, she told herself. It was, after all, just the beginning and Rafael seemed open to talking about his story. Maybe she'd be walking out on her first real challenge as a writer. Yet more important, she might be walking out on him, leaving behind the opportunity to tell his story in his own words.

Elena closed her eyes and drifted off into half sleep, but she was startled awake when she realized that Rafael was standing by her side looking down at her. She sat up and looked around, unsure if she had napped.

"It's gettin' cold out here. Let's go into the game room. It's empty now."

"Fine. Help me with my things."

Elena and Rafael made their way back into the main house and into the large room. She looked around, taking in the card tables, chairs, and a Ping-Pong stand set up close to one of the corners. Rafael led the way to a couple of overstuffed chairs separated by a small magazine table. He put down the recorder and her briefcase and then he plopped down on one of the chairs waiting for her to do the same. Almost as an afterthought, he turned to her.

"Wanna cup of coffee?"

"Yes."

Rafael shuffled toward a small room where Elena watched him fix the instant coffee. She settled into the chair prepared for another session, knowing that she had made her decision to go on.

"I lived cooped up with my ol' man till I was four years ol'. He didn't let me visit Abuela or my aunts, and he gave the cops orders to keep all of my mother's family away from me."

"Was he afraid they might hurt you?"

"He was a bastard. I think he wanted to punish them."

"For what?"

"Because they was family to Rosario, I guess. I can't remember stayin' with nobody for Christmas or Easter or picnics, not till I was about five years ol' when Abuela and the family scraped up enough money to get a lawyer to help out.

"When I thinka them days I know the cops had it all wrong. It was livin' with my ol' man—that freaked me out. Jesus! I was so scared of him and his big fancy house. I was even spooked by the broads he shacked up with, they was so goddamn ugly. The only good thing was that they came and went, but even them bitches didn't scare me as much as nighttime. I was afraid of the night and the dark when the crazy nightmares came as soon as I went to sleep."

Rafael stopped speaking while Elena studied him. He examined her, too, looking intently at her as if trying to discover what was going on inside of her. She returned his hard stare, holding his eyes with hers for a long time.

"Wanna hear about them nightmares?"

"Go ahead."

"I had a bunch of 'em, but two of 'em ran around after me just about every night and I still don't know which one scared me the most. There was the one where I saw myself plugged right through the head. It happened in the pitch-black night. In that dream I could see a stinkin' dried up ol' hand come outta the wall. The ugly twisted thing grabbed a gun that clicked and clicked and then blew out my brains. Splat! Brains all over the wall."

The image of brains splattered on the wall made Elena's stomach churn. She hated hearing about it and did not want to listen to more of the ugly description. Rafael caught the expression on her face and guessed what she was thinking.

"It's part of my life. I can't go on without tellin' you what I went through when I was a kid. Okay? Each time I woke up after that dream I screamed out my guts, but nobody ever came, not the maid, not one of the broads, much less my ol' man. Papá! Papá! I used to sit stiff and shiverin' in the bed, my shorts drippin' with pee. Papá! Papá! But each time I knew nobody was comin', so I scrambled outta bed, pulled a blanket on the floor, and rolled up on top of it. I was so scared the hand would come outta the wall all over again I tried to keep awake, but no matter how much I tried, I drifted off again and the crap started all over.

"There was another nightmare that spooked the crap outta me for years. It started after the time my ol' man took me to school for the first time. He got me all excited about it; he even gave me a buncha toys. He told me that I was a big guy now and I needed to be real smart, just like him. So I got all jazzed up, but when the big fat teacher sat me at her desk and started pilin' books and pencils on top of me I freaked out. Don't ask me why I got so scared, I just did and I started to cry. I mean it was serious, wide-open, tongue-stickin-outta-mouth bawlin'.

"When I started that racket my ol' man told me to pipe down but I just squealed more. Then he lost it. He grabbed me by the shoulders and shook the hell outta me but the more he yelled, the more I howled.

Shut up! Shut up! Goddamn it! I said shut your trap! If you don't pipe down, I'm sending you to the slammer with your ol' lady. You'll be locked up behind bars until the guards come to stretch your neck! Shut up!

"Bastard! I don't know why the hell he did that. What I do remember is that I stopped bawlin' even if inside I was cavin' in 'cause I was so goddamn scared. Honest to God, I thought I was gonna drown in somethin' nasty that was stuffin' my mouth, my nose, and even my eyes. I'll tell you that I clammed up so tight that I couldn't hardly talk to nobody after that.

"The baddest part of the whole thing was the nightmare that came to me almost every night after that day. The only good part about it was that it shoved away the other dream. In this nightmare I was the one who pulled the trigger that whacked my brother and sisters. I was the one! Nobody else! I was the one who done the murders all along! In the dream I got everythin' all mixed up. I was the one who went to the slammer where I was put behind big bars, waitin' and waitin' to have my neck stretched till it got to be three feet long.

"That nightmare freaked me out all the time and I pissed all over the bed night after night. Even now the memory sticks in my throat. Christ! I still get so screwed up just thinkin' about it that I almost mess my pants as ol' as I am."

"Rafael, what about the other dream you described yesterday? In that one you're not the killer. It's somebody else."

"That's right."

"Well, what about it?"

"What do you mean?"

"I mean that it's got to be one or the other."

"I don't know. Everythin' gets all mixed up in my head."

"Rafael, let's stop here. I think you've told me enough for the time being."

"Are you gettin' chicken on me?"

"No. I'm tired."

"You hated hearin' about the nightmares."

"Yes. They're awful but that doesn't mean that I don't want us to go on with our interviews. All I can say is that you have to remind yourself that you didn't kill your brother and sisters and that you're not responsible for any part of it. No one is going to kill you."

"Maybe it was me who whacked them."

"Stop it! You were a baby!"

"That's what everybody says but maybe it was just part of the big lie."

"Rafael, it was your mother who did it."

"No! She's innocent, goddamn it!"

Elena stood up abruptly and began to gather her things. She felt her head pounding with fatigue and anxiety. Rafael's intensity had rubbed off on her; she knew that she needed separation right away.

"I'll return tomorrow."

"No you won't."

"I'll come after your breakfast. Be ready."

"I have a lotta stuff to tell you."

"I'm sure you do. In the meantime, we both need to rest. I'll see you tomorrow."

With briefcase and purse under her arm, Elena headed toward the door. Before she went through it she turned back to look at Rafael standing where she had left him. He was staring at her and something inside of her moved. For a moment she thought that it was pity but then she knew that it was doubt about his mother's guilt. And that misgiving was growing, getting bigger and disturbing her more than anything else.

When Elena got to her apartment she peeled off her clothes and went straight to the bathroom where she stood under the shower for a long time. Her head was buzzing with Rafael's words and images. His voice was stuck inside her just as vividly as it had been that afternoon. She shut off the water but she remained in the stall naked and dripping, still thinking. She finally stepped out and got into the terry-cloth robe that was hanging behind the door.

With wet hair wrapped in a towel and in bare feet, she shuffled to the kitchen. She put on the kettle thinking that a cup of tea would settle her nerves. While the water came to a boil she checked the fridge thinking that even if she was not hungry, eating might help her shake off what she was feeling. She pulled out some leftover tuna salad, slapped it between two slices of bread, and then stared at the sandwich for a long time, wondering if she would really eat the thing. Hoping to make it more appetizing, she pulled out an open bag of chips but after nibbling on one she pushed the whole thing aside—they were too stale to eat.

When the kettle spouted off, Elena began to prepare the tea but then stopped, deciding that she wanted something else. She opened the cupboard to the pint of scotch whiskey she had on hand. She poured a double shot and splashed water into it. Plate and glass in hand, she went to the small living room and plopped down on the easy chair in front of the television set.

Eyes closed, she tried to relax her body by leaning her head against the headrest but she could not shake off the deep feelings of sadness and confusion. She took a long gulp from the glass, grabbed the remote, and clicked on the news. Elena stared at the screen, vaguely aware of the day's late-breaking news: traffic snarls because of Christmas shoppers, the robbery at the 7-11, a man telling of what he would do if he won the lotto.

In a few minutes the images began to fade and Rafael's face and voice emerged. Elena shook her head hoping to clear it, trying to erase what she was experiencing. How would she be able to write the story if her emotions were getting the better of her? She had to find a way to separate her feelings from the facts of the case. She had to remember all those details she knew almost by heart. Rosario Cota was guilty. That was all there was to it! Period! The case had been tried years ago. Rosario was found guilty and, poor thing, she would soon be paying for it. From that point onward readers would be interested in only one thing written by Elena: how Rosario's son was coping with such a nightmare.

Elena drained the glass, wolfed down the sandwich, turned off the television and lamp, and headed to bed. Forcing herself not to think, she got under the covers, rolled over on her side, and fell into fitful sleep.

CHAPTER 4

The weather had turned chilly so Elena and Rafael decided to sit in the game room as they had the evening before. From where she sat she watched nurses taking a break as they stood by the coffee machine gossiping. She relaxed in the chair, enjoying the warmth of the pale sun filtering in through the large windows. At the same time she kept an eye on Rafael, sensing that he was in a mood different from the day before.

"Are you feeling okay?"

"Yeah. Why?"

"You seem different today."

"I'm cool."

"Fine. Let's get to work. I'd like to know about your days growing up, how things went in school for you and, if you'd like to talk about it, how you got along with your father."

A sudden loud snorting startled Elena. When she looked at him, Rafael's eyes were filled with mockery as he pressed both hands to his mouth and nose as if suppressing laughter. She saw that it was a fake gesture but she got the message, so she decided not to push the subject. Instead she kept quiet until he decided to speak.

"Everything was pretty much the same when I was a kid. At night I got all frazzled by the nightmares, then in the morning the maid came to make me take a bath and get dressed. I hated that bitch! She gave me the same crappy line every morning.

More pee? What's your Papá gonna say?

"What did the ol' man say? It's what he done that counted. He whipped my ass somethin' awful each time, like his

33

belt would plug up the piss. It didn't, and the bangin' kept up for years. On top of that he dragged me to some sonofabitch shrink. Right away, that dickhead gave me a buncha pills to swallow. I had some kinda ding-dong problem, he said. If anybody woulda asked me, I woulda told 'em that he was the one with the problem. If you coulda smelt him the way I had to, you'd puke right here on my lap. He stunk like a dead dog. I hated him almost as much as I hated my ol' man, but I got even with him when he gave me the shitty pills. Guess what I did with 'em?"

Rafael gawked at Elena, a mischievous look pasted on his face. His hands were twitching, flitting from his face, hair, and then down to his knees. He licked his lips as if reliving those unhappy moments of his life, but Elena kept quiet.

"Sometimes I swallowed the stinkin' thing but most times I put it under my tongue and when nobody was lookin' I spit it out. The one or two times that I did scarf it down I felt rotten, like my feet was bricks and my head filled with buzzin' flies. I wanted to sleep, that was all, so I hated the goddamn things. But guess what? When I didn't pass the stuff I got all jiggly and hyper, like I was about to scratch the walls or maybe jump all over the teacher's ugly face.

"One day the feelin' inside me got so big that I just couldn't stand it. So I got the idea of runnin' up and down between desks knockin' over books. I wanted to do it so bad that I just couldn't hold back. So I did it. God! I loved it! I ran up to the big board and started throwin' erasers at the kids and even at the fat bitch teacher. Most of the kids thought it was real cute and some of 'em even started throwin' stuff around. You shoulda seen it after a while! It was a circus and no matter how much the King Kong teacher shouted and waved her arms tryin' to get all them snots under control, she couldn't. She lost it and I loved it.

"She tried to put me down but I turned into a wild mule, kickin' and bitin'. My arms was spokes that swung round and my legs was jabbin' pistons, but at last she was able to pick me up and she threw me outta the room. I laughed like a hyena when I landed on my ass. I didn't give a shit what she done to me. I knew she was scared outta her gourd and that made me feel good.

"Oh, yeah! I went on a rampage that day. It was the first time but not the last. I kept on doin' it. After them blowouts I didn't need nobody, even if I was punished somethin' awful. My ol' man forced me to go back each time. I guess he paid the school or somethin', why else did they keep me? I hated the teachers, the kids, the rooms, everythin'. I even hated the books so much that I kicked 'em around my room when I was alone.

"What I remember about them years is that I felt alone, real alone, especially when the other kids bragged about their brothers and sisters and how they played games in their yards or in the garage. Little shithead punks! I hated all of 'em! When I went home after school all I had was the stinkin' cartoons on television and I hated 'em, too!"

Rafael stopped speaking and looked at Elena who appeared not to be listening to him. She was gazing out the window, her eyes following the gardener as he mowed the lawn. Rafael flopped back in the chair frowning.

"I guess the goddamn machine is hearing my story even if you ain't."

"What do you mean?"

"I got eyes. I can see you ain't hearin' what I'm sayin'."

"I *am* listening. I'm thinking that if someone had paid attention to you when you were so little, maybe things might have turned out different for you."

"Just like you're payin' attention to me now?"

Stung by Rafael's sarcasm, Elena glared at him, resentful at being misunderstood. She reached for the recorder and clicked it off, convinced that they should take time off. However, she was taken off guard when he snatched the machine from her hands, punched it back on, and without explaining or even looking at her, he began to speak into the microphone.

"I got more to say to this machine. I pulled that stunt a lotta times but it wasn't till later, when a buncha scumbag brats started to make fun of me about how my ol' lady snuffed out my brother and sisters. That's when I got freaked out and I let 'em have it. It happened when they got together and started singin' a little song one of them dickheads made up. They clapped their dirty hands and pulled a cute dance step, all the time singin' and laughin' like a buncha fuckin' monkeys.

One little cholo, Zap!
Two little cholas, Zap! Zap!
No more little cholos, Zap! Zap! Zap!

"At first, I felt stiff and ashamed. I didn't know what it was all about but it wasn't too long before I caught on. When they first got into it, I told 'em to shut up but they laughed and did it more. They did it over and over till I lost it and I didn't give 'em no chance to sing their lousy song again. I screamed, jumped 'em, my fists flyin'. I kicked, pulled hair, scratched and bit like a crazy dog. Jab! Jab! Them little bastards was scared shitless! Some of 'em slithered away but others ducked with their ugly heads hidin' behind their arms and a couple thought they could fight back. Them's the ones I mauled and when I was finished they looked like dog meat gone bad."

Elena watched as Rafael relived the fight. He sat on the edge of the chair shadowboxing unseen assailants, pumping his fists in midair, jabbing, ducking, feigning, and bobbing his head in an invisible bout. He swerved from side to side and then pressed forward, making hissing noises through clenched teeth. Finally, when he realized that she was staring at him, he dropped his fists onto his lap and stopped moving.

He wiped his forehead and cheeks and turned to look out the window, calming down as if nothing had happened.

"That blowout happened when we was on recess and it wasn't till the yard teacher made it through the mob of yellin' kids that I stopped but it was too late. There was a lotta busted lips and fat cheeks by the time he got to us. I even tried to take on that big gorilla teacher but I was too little and he was too big. But I gave him hell and he hadda pick me up before he could take me to the principal's office, kickin' and bitin'."

Rafael stopped speaking when he noticed Elena's expression. He narrowed his eyes, giving her a hard look.

"What? You think I'm puttin' you on?"

"No. I'm trying to understand what's so special about that fight. I'm sure you had others."

"Oh, yeah! I can't even count 'em but that one was important. It was the first time them twerps got up the nerve to make fun of what happened to my brother and sisters. That day was special, too. It was when I was kicked outta the goddamn school, even after my ol' man came and argued and promised a buncha things. This time the fat bitch teacher won. She told the principal that it was me or her. She couldn't stand me and she won. I didn't give a damn. I hated her too. You can erase this goddamn thing if you think I'm lyin', but you asked me about them days, so there it is."

"I don't think you're lying. I'm just sorry it happened that way."

"Well, being sorry don't mean jackshit. What's important is that I started to see that my ol' man was a rich big shot. I could tell by how all them flunkies acted when he went to meet with them.

Yes, Mr. Cota. No, Mr. Cota. Can I kiss your ass, Mr. Cota?

"Them brown noses didn't say nothin' more. Suckin' up to the ol' man was in their eyes. I could tell even if I was just a twerp, but the day came when his money didn't count for shit. Them teachers and principals just couldn't stand me no more. So it was, *Out on your ass, little Rafael.* Not much has changed since."

"Rafael, how old were you when this happened?"

"About nine or ten."

"Didn't you have friends?"

"Nope! It wasn't till later when I started hangin' with the valley *cholos.* That's when I wasn't no lone coyote no more."

"Which valley?"

"Yours. San Fernando."

"How did you get down there?"

"Hey! Hang on to your shorts. That's comin'."

"Okay. I'll be patient. In the meantime, what did your father do all those years when you were a kid?"

"Nothin'."

"Yesterday you said that when you were about five you began to visit your grandmother. What about those days?"

Rafael smiled broadly and his eyes suddenly filled with light, transforming his face. Elena, taken by surprise by yet another change in him, blinked, wondering if this was the same sullen man who had spoken so bitterly of poisonous memories, of hating teachers, kids, books, the maid, and even his father.

"Them was good days for me. I got permission to spend my summer vacations with her. I loved that time and the way Abuela talked and the food she made and the stories she told. She lived in a house different from my ol' man's mansion. It was a little frame house on the street next to a field where crops grew: artichokes, tomatoes, beans, onions. She had her own garden where she planted vegetables that I watered. When the squash, tomatoes, and chilies was ripe, she let me pick 'em off the vines.

"At the end of the day we sat on the rickety porch to watch the sun go down. Now, when I'm feelin' real bummed, I think back to them days real hard and I still pick up the good smell of strawberries that drifted toward us from that long field. It was there that we sat, covered with all kinds of sounds and colors. We talked a lot but most of all I tuned in to what she said.

"By that time Abuela was livin' alone. Abuelo was dead and all her kids was married or livin' in different places, but I could tell that outta all of 'em, Rosario was the one planted deep in Abuela's heart. It was always about her that we ended up talkin'. She told me stories of when Rosario was a little girl and she never got tired of tellin' me how much I looked like her when she was my age. Then she'd pull out her pictures just to prove to me how much I looked like her. Abuela sometimes cried and then hugged me real close, almost always sayin' the same thing.

Your Mamá is in prison waiting to die but she's innocent. I hope she'll still be with us by the time you grow up. It'll be up to you to prove that she's innocent. You're the one, mi'ijito. You're the one.

I wanna see her, Abuela.

As soon as you're grown up, mi'ijito.

"Abuela had a lotta pictures of Rudy and the girls. It was about that time that I found out that the kids loved softball, that they played on teams all the time, and that Rosie was already famous for her pitchin' arm. There was one picture of the kids just around the time they died. They was wearin' baseball shirts with their name on it and they was smilin' great big smiles, like their team just won the game.

"I was little the first time I saw that picture. I asked Abuela to show it to me all the times I went to her place. I was crazy about it and as the years went by I saw that I got older and bigger but the kids stayed the same. I still feel weird thinkin' that I'm a man and they're still little kids stuck in the picture, happy 'bout winnin' a game."

The recorder shut off. Elena replaced the tape and pushed the record button, then she looked at Rafael astonished that the change that had come over him was not momentary. His voice was low, his words were gentle, his eyes were not hostile anymore, and his mouth was soft and smiling. She thought that it was as if a mask had been peeled off his face, letting her see a different person beneath it. Fearing that she might say something to jolt him back into anger, she silently motioned with her hand for him to go on speaking.

"It wasn't just pictures and talk of Rosario that filled up them days. Abuela told me stories of the olden times in Mexico when she was a little girl and she went out to the fields with the rest of the family on picnics. She used to get happy when she talked this way, tellin' me about how they rode burros all over the place and when they got tired they cooked meat and tortillas in a fire built over a hole dug in the dirt. Hey! I'll bet your folks are from down there, too. Right?"

Rafael's question was so unexpected that it took Elena a few seconds to respond. She was caught off guard again by his switching the focus from himself to her, so she took a few seconds to answer.

"Yes. My mom is from Zacatecas and dad is from Sonora."

"They still alive?"

"Yes."

"Do they talk English?"

"Yes. They came to this country when they were young."

"Was they married?"

"No. They met here and married after that."

"Do you live with 'em?"

"No."

"Why not?"

"I need privacy."

Rafael wrinkled his brow as if not understanding, but then sighed and closed his eyes, lost in thought. Elena sensed how deeply he hungered to know more about her. Something told her that he wanted to know what it was like to live with a mother and a father and that he craved to hear of her life with a family.

"Do you want to go on telling me about your grandmother?"

"Yeah. What I loved about her stories was the legends. There was the one about the Devil and how that bugger came around shaped like a beautiful babe, just to jump in front of a disobedient son. When the guy tried to take her in his arms to smooch, she turned ugly, with fangs just like the Devil. That taught the dude a lesson real good and he never disobeyed his mother again. But there was other legends that Abuela told me and I never forgot none of 'em. The one that sticks with me the most is the one she called La Llorona. You heard about it?"

"Yes. It's about the woman who never stops crying."

"Right. I don't know if it's for real or if Abuela was talkin' about Rosario. The story is about a woman who popped her kids outta vengeance when her husband was fuckin' around. Abuela concentrated on this story but it was kinda screwy. She changed it a little bit every time she told it. Sometimes the kids was drowned, another time they was strangled, or maybe they was poisoned. Whatever happened, in the end the kids died and it was their mom who done it. There was only one thing that made me think that Abuela wasn't talkin' about Rosario. In the legend the mother didn't go to no prison. Instead, she hung around forever, howlin' and screechin' 'cause she was so sorry for what she done.

"Abuela said that even if this happened a long time ago in Mexico, at night people in different places still heard that weird woman wailin'. She said she even knew some people who swore they heard the woman cryin', not once but a lotta times. She said that not miles or no borders could keep out La Llorona and it was for sure that in a single night the howlin' could be heard down in Mexico and then, almost at the same time, up here in the onion fields of the Salinas Valley."

Rafael stopped speaking and gazed through the window. His face now had taken on a sad expression. Elena did not want to interrupt him, so she sat quietly trying to decipher his thoughts, baffled by the complexity she continued to discover in him. When minutes passed and he still remained withdrawn, she decided to end the session.

"Let's call it a day, Rafael."

"Hey! Hang on! There's just a little bit more I wanna tell. It's about Abuela and what we did before we went to bed. She stopped her stories after it got dark, when she looked up at the sky to see how high the stars was. Then we got back into the house where a small candle was always burnin'. Then we kneeled by my bed to pray and even if my knees hurt I never bellyached 'cause I liked the sound of her voice so much. I listened hard to hear her pray for all her kids, especially for Rosario.

"We prayed the rosary all the nights, one Hail Mary after the other one but I didn't ever finish the whole thing before I fell asleep, still on my knees, with my head and shoulders plopped against the bed like a sack of onions. When I woke up, Abuela had already put on my pajamas and got me under the covers. Then she'd kiss me on the cheek and say 'Good night, *mi'ijito*.' After that I'd fall asleep and dream all kindsa things like tomato vines and stars and a crazy woman who killed her kids and went around the world cryin' and cryin'."

CHAPTER 5

Before going in to see him the following morning, Elena sat in her car thinking of Rafael as a child. Again she thought of the old woman who planted the seed of Rosario's innocence so deeply in his mind that more than likely nothing could uproot it now. Elena wondered if it had been a crack in that belief that ultimately caused his mental breakdown. What if Rafael ever became fully convinced that his mother was indeed guilty? What would happen?

Elena put a stop to her thoughts because she disliked going down a road filled with suppositions. There was too much of Rafael's real life to write about, information that readers would find interesting without having to guess at what might have been. With this in mind, she gathered her things, stepped out of the car, and headed for the main building where she found Rafael waiting for her. Looking drained, he stood by the door leading to the back lawn. She thought that he probably had not slept well and although she felt a flash of pity for him she put on a cheerful look.

"Good morning."

"You're late!"

"I had a few last minute things to take care of."

"Like what?"

"Like checking in with my boss."

"Well, okay, but let's get to it. I have a lotta things I wanna tell you today. I wanna sit outside, so don't get cold again. You should wear the right stuff and not the cheesy things you always have on."

"I'm sorry you don't approve of how I dress."

"Aw, forget it. Sit here. Where's the goofy machine?"

Rafael's crankiness exasperated Elena but she resisted the feeling as she took the chair and opened her briefcase. She also noticed that Rafael was becoming more familiar with her, more demanding, and she did not like it. Again putting aside her resentment she set up the recorder and signaled that she was ready to go on, but he kept quiet as he glared at her.

"Well? How do you 'spect me to know where the hell to begin?"

"Rafael! Why are you being so nasty? Start wherever you want. How about when you were a teenager."

"Okay, but don't get bitchy with me or I'll just clam up and there goes your goddamn story right down the toilet."

"Look, let's start all over again so we can get off on the right foot. You left off telling of your days with your grandmother. Why not pick up there? What was it like when you returned to your father's place?"

"What do you think? I hated everythin'. I felt so bummed I didn't even wanna get outta bed. The big rooms and the slippery tile floors made me feel like crap. It took me a long time to get used to the empty rooms in the ol' man's mansion after my visits with Abuela and by the time I was gettin' used to that dump, it was time to go back to her house. That went on till she died.

"School? I was in and outta them places more times than I can remember. I ditched nearly every day and I lied to the ol' man about goin' to classes but there was always some scumbag stoolie that spilled the beans. The ol' man finally got so pissed that he almost threw me outta the house, but it didn't make no difference to me. I was on the streets most of the time anyway."

Rafael rubbed his hands, crossed and uncrossed his legs, then began to nibble on his fingernails. Elena waited until he was ready to go on. When he spoke, his voice was soft.

"You wanna know about me and girls? Well, I didn't have no serious girl. Honest to God, I didn't know nothin' about how to act with 'em. I'm not sayin' that I didn't fuck. I did, lotsa times. I just didn't get serious with nobody. I felt too stiff, too stupid, and this pissed me off so much that sometimes I even beat the crap outta some of them bitches after I finished with them.

"God! When I did that, I thought of Abuela and even Rosario and what they woulda thought of me. This feelin' got me so ashamed that I'd try to hide. I didn't want 'em to see what a pig I was. I'd drag my ass off to some alley where there was just a buncha stinkin' garbage cans and me and there I'd bawl like a goddamn baby. I woulda given anythin' to tell Abuela how sorry I was but she was gone by that time.

"I was about fifteen by then and all I did was hang around with the other losers in the barrio. It was then that I started gettin' the screwy idea that I had to see Rosario and I remembered that I wanted to do that since the happy days with Abuela. But now, the more I thought about it, the bigger the feelin' got inside me. I couldn't understand why I never seen her 'cept in pictures. I didn't know where to start or how to get permission to visit her. So I thought that maybe this one time the ol' man would help me out. But goddamn it! The only thing I got outta him was a bad mouth. That's when we had our first big blowout.

"That day I found him in the kitchen havin' drinks and I could tell that he wasn't feelin' no pain. He had that ugly pink look pasted on his mug. As soon as he seen me he started the ol' bullshit about how it was Rosario who whacked the kids. That was nothin' new. He used to do that all the time 'cause he saw how it pissed me to hear him say that, but this time I tried to hang on to the horses. I thought I could get his help, but after a while I lost it.

How can I see Rosario?

¿Qué? ¡Pendejo! ¡Salte de aquí!

Don't gimme that crap! Talk so I can understand! I said I wanna see her!

45

What for? She murdered your brother and sisters!
No she didn't!
When will you finally get it through your head? Your mother is a murderer!
Liar! She's innocent!
Who told you that?
Abuela!
That old bag!

"I swear that when he said that about Abuela I felt sick, like I had pigged out on booze and crappy food. I felt like I was gonna puke right there, but instead it was filthy words that came outta my mouth.

Shut up, motherfucker! I'm sick and tired of you talkin' that way.
What did you say?
You heard me. Lay off Abuela and Rosario!
Punk! You can't talk to me that way.
I am talkin' that way. So what're you gonna do about it?
Get the hell out of here!
I'm outta here but first lemme tell you that I know Rosario didn't do it.
What's that supposed to mean?
It means that I know who killed the kids and it wasn't her.
You're crazy!
I ain't crazy and you know it.
I said get the hell out of here.

"I could tell that all that yellin' got to him. It was the first time I bucked him. I didn't move. I just kept eyeballin' him, lettin' him know that now I was big enough to take him on. No more belts bangin' up my ass. I stared at him till my eyeballs hurt, waitin', waitin', wantin' him to ask me who snuffed out the kids. I wanted that to happen so bad that my guts got on fire and my mouth filled up so bad that I spit out a big goober, right there on his fancy floor. But even that didn't get him to ask me the big question. The ol' fart just kept clammed up, scared outta his gourd. So I spun around and walked outta that house. After that I went back sometimes only to sleep."

"He didn't help you?"

"Nope."

"Did you find another way to see her?"

"Yeah. One day after that I got gutsy enough to walk into a police station and I asked the first guy in uniform what I should do. At first he looked at me like I was a freak or somethin', but then he told me to sit down, give him Rosario's name and what prison she was in. He asked me why she was put away. I think he felt sorry for me after I told him and after a while he told me what to do."

"Then what?"

"There was a paper I filled out and mailed to the pen where she was holed up. It wasn't no big deal. Just my name, some dates, and why I wanted to see Rosario."

"Well?"

"I waited till I got the answer."

"So you did see your mother when you were a kid."

"Nope."

"I don't understand."

"I didn't see her. She didn't wanna see me."

"I still don't understand. Why wouldn't she want to see you?"

"How am I supposed to know? I'm sayin' that she didn't wanna see me! How come you don't understand that?"

Elena saw that Rafael had become so agitated that he was close to tears. His voice was cracking and his chest heaving; she realized that she had crossed a line. She backed away, waiting for him to overcome the emotions assaulting him.

"Not long after I got the bad news from Rosario I walked outta the ol' man's mansion and I drifted from one place to the other, workin' different jobs, sleepin' here or there, hoppin' on freight trains that took me up and down the state. I made my way south to the San Joaquin Valley and even as far down to Imperial County where I hitched up with a buncha wetbacks. They helped me a lot, especially when I hit the fields harvestin' beans and other stuff all the way up to King City, then way down to Santa Paula, but I quit after a couple of seasons. There was no way I coulda kept up with them guys. Their backs and arms was as tough as the hoes they swung up and down like goddamn pistons.

"From Santa Paula I stayed on the move south till I landed in your turf, the San Fernando Valley, where I hit the streets and hung out with other barrio losers, sleepin' where they slept, scarfin' up whatever came around. Most of the time I scrounged up enough bread liftin' hubcaps or connin' Chink merchants outta food. Sometimes I got by on a dime or a quarter. I spent days in pool halls or on street corners where I picked up on smokin' and boozin' and hangin' with homie girls. All the time piss was boilin' inside me 'cause Rosario had turned me down. I didn't give a damn about the ol' man, but her, that was different, and the more I thought about it the more I wanted to see her.

"I cussed out anybody who got close to me. I acted like a wild dog with the guys, but that was only on the outside 'cause on the inside I felt my heart rollin' up like a ball. It was about that time that I started thinkin' a lot about the kids and how they'd been snuffed out and that a good-for-nothin' bastard like me was still alive and kickin'.

"Jesus! Thinkin' this way pretty much drove me outta my gourd. I told myself that this was why Rosario didn't wanna see me. And who could blame her? Some asshole came along and killed her kids but left a little creep like me behind. Who could deal with that one? I couldn't blame her. No way!

"When I was around nineteen a weird thing started to happen to me. All that piss inside pushed me into a black pit and the feeling got so big that I stopped talkin'. I hung around street corners or just sat on empty crates thinkin' and thinkin' about Rosario and the kids. If anybody coulda looked inside me, they would've seen a hole filled with stinkin' mud. I swear to you that it got so bad that I could hardly move one leg in front of the other one.

"Then one day, when the guys forced me to hang with them, I felt my heart start to pound. I thought I was chokin' and that I was gonna croak. It got so bad that I could hardly breathe and I got spooked but the more scared I got, the more messed up I got. Then I started to hack and wheeze but them stupid bums didn't do jackshit 'cept stand around laughin' at me. They thought I was pullin' a cute joke. They started to shout that I sounded like a broken down jalopy.

"That was the first time but that crap hit me other times and each time I passed out like a two-bit wino caved in on a park bench. The guys kept on thinkin' it was just a joke till the time my eyes started screwin' up and down, then they stopped laughing. They didn't know what to do till someone thought of splashin' my face with some leftover shitty beer.

"After that the feelin' happened all the time and each time I got more spooked. It hit me at weird times when I was off guard. The feelin' started in my heart and then shot down to my guts. Next it knifed over to my lungs and, sure thing, there I was, one passed out scumbag, gurglin' and jigglin' my legs in the air, right there in front of everybody.

"Then I started to think that Rudy, Rosie, and even Connie was followin' me, pushin' me, wantin' to say somethin'. Voices banged up my brain, sayin' this, sayin' that. I boozed a lot tryin' to forget the crazy shit but the voices got worse. I passed out more times and I was feelin' so messed up that I was sure I was losin' my marbles. The guys started to nag me, even whispering behind my back and after a time almost shoutin', *Go to a bruja! Go to a shrink! Do this! Do that! Blah, blah, blah!*

"I knew I hadda do somethin'. At first I thought of runnin' away but didn't have nowhere to escape and in the meantime months passed while the thing kept happenin'. I hated hangin' with all those losers. I couldn't stand their big burro laughs no more, so I slunk away. At first I disappeared little by little, then more and more days passed till I went alone to a corner of the Valley where nobody could find me.

"I kept thinkin' that the voices in my head was the kids tellin' me somethin' but I couldn't be sure. What if it was the voice of some asshole tryin' to drive me crazy? The god-damned chatter kept bangin' all the time and nothin' stopped it 'cept booze. Only when I was smashed could I rest just a little bit."

Rafael leaned his head on the backrest and closed his eyes while Elena gazed at him, admitting that his intensity was intimidating her. She felt that she could handle knowing of the addictions that had plagued him and even his abusive behavior but hearing voices was something else; this part scared her. It occurred to her that she was tampering with something dangerous and that she might be getting in over her head. Grateful for his silence, she took the time to sort out her thoughts. After a while she decided that this might be the time to forget about the interviews and cut off their encounters.

"Rafael, why don't we end our meetings?"

"What?"

"I think I've heard enough of your story. We can end it now."

"You mean for always?"

"Yes."

"We can't stop now! I have too much to tell you."

"I don't want you to get sick over this. It's not worth it."

"It *is* worth it! You can't walk out on me! Nothin' can stop me now, so get used to it!"

"I don't know, Rafael. I think I should speak to some-one."

"To who?"

"Your doctor."

"That's bullshit! We don't need that dickhead stickin' his nose into what we're doin'. Let's just go on with our business, or maybe you're gettin' chicken."

Elena, wondering if he was reading her thoughts, refused to respond. Instead she got to her feet and gathered her things. He, too, got up and stood so close to her that she felt his breath on her face.

"If that's what you want, Rafael, but I've had it for today. I need to rest. I'll come back tomorrow."

CHAPTER 6

"I was a hobo sleepin' in alleyways, hangin' around streets and eatin' handouts I scrounged up. My hair was mangy and wild, just like my beard. My clothes was rags, stuff that I dug outa dumpsters and most times I didn't have no shoes to wear. Christ! I was about twenty, but I musta looked like a starved ol' mutt. When I dragged myself out to streets where nice people hung out, they took a look at me and then made a U-turn. I spooked 'em real bad. All the time the crap inside my head kept makin' me pass out but now nobody paid no attention. I was just one more drunk spread out on a sidewalk."

Rafael spoke softly into the recorder. It was raining that morning so he and Elena were back in the game room. As she listened to him, she gazed out at the lawn and trees, watching droplets tracing crooked paths down the windowpane. Everything looked gray and trees blurred like jagged silhouettes.

"I hitched up with the gangs of freaks that hang around the Valley streets but after a while I ended up in the middle of L.A. I don't remember how the hell that happened, it just did. When I found out; I was glad 'cause that part of town has places that give free handouts. It's a buncha charity houses that give a guy a bed for the night, food, and even a shower, but it happens only with a lotta luck.

"So I was just one more smashed or stoned loser who ripped off other scumbags just to get junk to keep goin'. Sometimes when I felt strong I grabbed a cardboard box or even a piece of canvas to crawl under to sleep. Most times I had to beat up somebody to get that stuff. All us bums did it, there's nothin' much different about that."

"Why didn't you go back to your father? He would have helped you."

"Are you crazy? He wouldn't do jackshit to help me. Anyway, that's the last thing I would've done. What I wanted real bad was to croak. Down deep I hoped that some dickhead would smash my brains out while he was fuckin' me or maybe I coulda kicked the bucket. But I didn't. I kept on livin'."

Elena stared at Rafael, caught up by what he had just said. Had he been assaulted sexually or had she heard it wrong? She put up her hand, signaling him to stop speaking.

"Rafael, were you attacked sexually?"

"Yeah! A lotta times. It happens just about every day to most bums. I can't even remember how many times it came down on me, but I'll tell you that it happens not only to guys. Females that drag their ass through those streets get hit even more. It don't make no difference if you're a bitch or some slime bucket, everybody gets the hit sooner or later. Which means that everybody makes hits right back. You get what I mean?

"If you wanna know the truth about them days in my life, I have to tell you about one time when it was my turn to make the hit. The reason I remember that time is 'cause it was a real ugly fight over a goddamn cardboard box. It was more than a fight. What I remember first is a shape comin' at me. Then I hear some mixed-up words and after that comes the big one, a nasty, mean tangle.

"Some sonofabitch started eyeballin' my cardboard and at first we just started pushin' each other around, but then it got big and both of us ended up rollin' on the ground, all slimy with rotten garbage and piss. I slugged at the bum, bitin' and gougin'. I cussed the motherfucker up and down, kickin' and scratchin', but when I thought I was losin' I cut loose with one last kick right into that soft gut.

GRACIELA LIMÓN

"I heard the asshole grunt and I knew I'd won. After that there was a lotta breathin' but I didn't know if it was the loser or me, so in a while I forced my eyes to open up. At first it was a big blur, then I seen that it was a bitch that I beat up. I stared and stared at her, beginnin' to think that maybe I done some chickenshit thing, but then I told myself that she started it. Then she got to puking real hard, so I crawled away till she got done. The stink was bad but I wasn't gonna walk away from my cardboard, so I waited."

"Did you help her?"

"What? Why should I help her? No! I fucked her."

Elena, who had not slept well and had been fighting off a headache, now felt a throbbing pain behind her eyes so strong that it flattened her thoughts, compelling her to question what she was doing. Why should she go on listening to this miserable story? Why should she even write about it? What good could possibly come from it?

Disgusted, she rubbed her forehead and she was quiet for a while as she tried to put her finger on what exactly had triggered so much revulsion in her. After a few moments she knew. Rafael's foul mouth was too much for her. His constant cursing and slimy images caught up with her, sickening her. Above all, the abusive acts he had just described appalled her and she could not control the rage that spilled out when she spoke.

"Rafael, I'm fed up with your bad language. I know you've had a rough time, but enough is enough. I'm sick of your garbage-can mouth so if you want to go on with your story you'd better cut out the slime."

He gawked at her with an expression of complete surprise and he sat looking at her as if she were a creature from another planet. Stunned, he sucked in a gulp of air, shifting his butt in the chair.

"It's the only way I know how to talk."

"Change it!"

54

"Goddamn it! You tell me another way I can say that I fucked the bitch. Go on! You say it! No? You don't know how? Oh, what the hell! You can write it up any way you wanna. I don't give a damn."

"It's not only your foul language, Rafael, it's *what* you're saying that's even more disgusting. Aren't you ashamed of having violated that woman? People go to prison for what you did. And why? For a piece of cardboard! You should feel rotten about what you did and at least take the blame."

"What're you talkin' about? It was her or me! You don't think she woulda done the same to me if she could've? It's the only way to keep alive on the streets! Everybody does it. Even you woulda done the same thing."

"No! I would not have done such a thing!"

"How do you know? You never been there."

"Rafael, aren't you sorry?"

"Sorry ain't got jackshit to do with it. It's about stayin' alive."

Their voices had escalated to a pitch that caused some of the patients to stare. Elena saw that one of the nurses had tensed, ready to take action, so she decided not to answer; she did not want to argue. Instead, she closed her eyes, trying to deflect the harsh blows his words were causing her and she struggled to get control of her emotions. She forced herself to understand that Rafael had lived a life more brutal than she could ever imagine. She told herself that she had to harden herself and listen to what he had to tell. It was his story and he was telling it the only way he knew, and if she was to be the writer she wanted to be, she had to step into his place. After a while she shrugged her shoulders, letting him know she accepted what he was saying. Rafael went on speaking as if nothing had happened.

"After that blowout, I don't remember nothin'. My memory shuts down tight and hard. All I know is that I hung around skid row for months lost in a black hole that made me a jailbird just like Rosario and all the time the voices kept on bangin' and bangin' whenever I came off a high.

"I don't know how long this went on but it did till one day when a goddamn car hit me while I staggered out into the middle of a street. It slammed me against the pavement and I was knocked out. When I woke up I was propped against a wall. I didn't know what the hell was happenin' even when I rubbed my eyes and shook my head. All I made out was knees passin' by me, some hoppin' over me, some trippin'. Only one guy stopped to say, *Hey, Buddy! You okay?* I stayed sprawled out on the ground. I just couldn't think straight.

"I don't know how many hours went by before thoughts started to pop up in my mind. I knew that I was lost. I know you think this is nuts but just knowin' that I was lost was a big deal for me after bein' so messed up for so long. That's when I started to straighten out. My next thought was that I didn't know what day it was, what month, or what year.

"No one bothered with me. A sprawled-out wino don't attract much attention in that part of town so I was left alone like I was a dead dog, 'cept I wasn't dead. Now I was more alive than dead. I was thinkin' real hard, tryin' to find somethin' I could remember but my head was empty so nothin' came to me no matter how much I tried. Only a few things floated inside me. I saw a hand givin' me a plate of food, then I saw the fight over the cardboard box and I saw the spread-out bitch. I didn't like what I saw but I hung on to them pictures. It was all I had.

"The longer I stayed there pasted to the wall the more I saw that I'd been lost like a goddamn alley cat. All of a sudden I felt spooked, more than when I was a kid. I was scared stiff 'cause I couldn't explain how I fell into that hole.

"I took a look at my skinny legs and saw that I was wearin' only one shoe and that the other foot was bare and smeared with slime, my nails was cracked and black with dirt. Then I saw that my pants was rags stiff with my own piss and crap. I started to gag and I went into dry heaves but nothin' came up, just a lotta hurt that made me see red spots.

"After it passed, I started hatin' myself. I was nothin' but a two-bit drunk, a bum, a loser. I thought again of Abuela and Rosario and I knew they wanted me to be one of the dead kids. I wanted to be dead like 'em, too. I wanted a bullet to come and blow my brains out.

"The bullet never came. That's when I knew that I had to get up and go somewhere. I didn't know where, just somewhere, but my legs was so goddamn wobbly that I had to hang on to walls, telephone poles, and garbage cans. I kept fallin', then crawlin' till someone finally took hold of my arm. *Come on, Buddy.* That voice is the last thing I remember before everythin' went black. When I woke up I saw a buncha bums, some scratchin' lice outta their hair, others passed out on cots, cryin' or grabbin' their gut. I was flat on my back and some guy was looking down at me.

You'll be okay. You're with the Brothers.

Whose brothers?

The Brothers of Charity. Do you think you're strong enough to stand up in a shower?

Yeah, if you gimme a hand.

"Christ! The feeling of water hittin' my shoulders felt like needles and I started to slip and slide but before I crashed on the floor, two hands came from I don't know where and held me up. Them same hands pulled me out, dried me, and covered me with clothes. They didn't let me fall into the cot, instead my hair and beard was buzzed, then I was plopped at a long table with the other zombies.

"A tin plate filled with what looked like slop was put in front of me, but just lookin' at it made me gag so I went to one of the Brothers and asked him to save the food for me. The guy knew what was happenin' to me so he took the plate without sayin' nothin'.

Brother, what day is it today?

December 3rd.
What year is it?
2000.

"It wasn't till then that I knew that I'd been lost for over a year and that I couldn't remember hardly nothin', not where I was, not what I did, not a goddamn thing, and I couldn't tell what kept me alive all that time.

"I was so spooked thinkin' about this that I started to faint again, so the Brother told me to hit the cot. I did and the last thing I remember is a lotta sniveling, grunts, moans, and snoring. Later on the guys told me that I stayed in the bed for days, all the time thrashin' and screamin' out for Rosario and Abuela. I'm glad that I don't remember any part of it 'cause I know that it hurts like hell gettin' rid of the poison. That's why I was screamin' my guts out."

Rafael got to his feet and moved close to the window, all the time stretching his legs and back. Elena reached over and shut off the recorder and she, too, stood up to take a break. She thought she would go outside to get air but saw that it was still raining, so she decided to stand by him until he was ready to go on. It was a while before he spoke.

"Do you think some asshole like me can change overnight?"

"What do you mean?"

"What I mean is that when I woke up from that ugly sleep I felt different, but I don't know if it happened then or later. I think it was right away, right there while I was still stretched out."

"Sometimes things happen that make us change. Are you talking about the car that nearly killed you?"

"Yeah! That, but even more when I found out that I'd been roamin' around garbage cans and alleyways and I didn't even know it. Knowin' that got me real scared. I even made a promise that it wouldn't happen again. Do you believe me?"

"Yes. I think I'd be scared too if I couldn't explain where I'd been for over a year."

Rafael returned to the chair and Elena did the same. She clicked on the recorder.

"I got to thinkin' that I was supposed to do somethin' special with my life and not just blow it away like it was a pile of crap. I thought and thought but I couldn't tell what that somethin' was. I couldn't come up with the answer right away so I thought I should give myself some time. All I knew was that I changed, that I didn't want to croak after all and that I had to live.

"I got outta the cot all wobbly and messed up but as the hours and days passed I got stronger. I knew that sooner or later I would leave the mission. There was other bums waitin' to take my place but I was spooked to go back out on them ugly streets. So I came up with a big idea. I asked the Brothers if I could stay on and work for my keep. There was a lotta work to do to keep that place goin'. You don't know how many poor bastards are out there and they just keep comin' and goin', all of 'em lost, polluted, all fucked up, so the mission is never empty.

"I got the green sign and stayed there workin' for more than a year. I washed dishes, scrubbed floors, put dirty towels and sheets in giant washin' and dryin' machines. I liked the work. It made me forget about the booze and other stuff like that. I started to get free and clean. I knew I was a new man. All that time I was the lone coyote, but I liked it. While I worked, my brain started to come together till I knew what I was supposed to do. After latchin' on to what that was, all I could do was to think about it and it got so big inside me that it almost burned me up."

"What about the voices that used to bug you? Did they disappear?"

"Yeah. The only voice that was left was Abuela's telling me that it was up to me to find out who really killed the kids."

Elena looked hard at him, shaking her head because she was more baffled than ever. Despite his life-threatening experiences out on the streets and even with his apparent inner conversion after that ordeal, Rafael still clung to the idea of his mother's innocence. Without trying to hide her exasperation, she spoke out.

"Rafael, have you ever tried to check on what really happened to your brother and sisters? I mean, have you read all the stuff that's out there? It might set you straight."

"Yeah, yeah, but don't start gettin' all bent outta shape again, okay? And what do you mean, *set me straight*? Everythin'I found proved that I was right."

"No, Rafael, you're only denying what happened and the longer you do that, the more hurt you'll get."

"Look, it's you that's got it all wrong. Anyway, do you wanna hear about it or not?"

"Go ahead."

"It started when I was still in the mission. A couple of the Brothers got real interested in my story after we rapped about it. I told 'em what I knew and how I felt it was up to me to prove that Rosario got a raw deal. They believed me and started to help me by gettin' me to read more. They knew that I dumped school, makin' me real bad at readin' and stuff like that. They gave me books, at first little ones about saints and other buggers. Then the things got bigger and more serious till I got pretty good at readin'."

"But you hadn't even seen your mother. Didn't the Brothers think that was important?"

"Yeah. They helped me with that, too. That's when I tried again to see Rosario and that time she said yes."

"You saw her?"

"Yeah."

"In San Quentin?"

"Right."

"Didn't you try to first find out what happened that night and during the trial?"

"While I waited to get the go-ahead from the prison I read all of that."

"Where? How?"

"The Brothers took me to a library and we dug up all the stuff. It was a buncha lies but I read that crap not once but over and over till I knew it by heart. It took me a long time but I got it straight."

"When did you see her? Recently?"

"Yeah, but only after I ran around findin' people who knew what happened that night."

"Like who?"

"Like the cop in charge of the investigation. Like the maid who was in the house that night. Like the ol' nun who got in tight with Rosario when she was waitin' for the trial."

"You talked to them?"

"Yeah."

"Are you going to tell me about it?"

"Yeah. That's what this is all about, ain't it?"

"Did those people give you different information?"

"Yeah."

"Like what?"

"Like none of 'em believe that Rosario committed the crime. 'Cept for the copper."

"What good did it do you except make you sick?"

"You're crazy! That's not what landed me here! It was somethin' else."

"Oh? What was that?"

"I'll tell you later."

"Rafael, I can't believe you looked up those people."

"What do you expect? I'm tellin' you that Rosario is innocent. They're plannin' to shove poison up her veins even though someone else popped the kids. The cops, the judge, the lawyers, the jury, even my ol' man, they all know it. So, who gives a shit if they make dog meat outta her. Right? Well, I do, that's for sure and I ain't givin' up."

Elena felt sick but she did not know if the nausea that was overcoming her was from extreme fatigue or from horror caused by thinking that a woman might be unjustly put to death. Her mind told her that this was impossible, that all the proof brought out in court showed, beyond a doubt, that Rosario Cota was guilty. On the other hand, what if she was innocent despite what appeared to be the truth? Elena got to her feet, at first unsteadily, but after regaining her balance she picked up her things and made for the door. Rafael followed her.

"Too bad I tol' you about the cardboard box."

"You were being honest."

CHAPTER 7

Elena returned to her apartment where she sat at the desk. She was worn out but she had changed into sweats and slippers and was beginning to feel relaxed. The headache that had begun as she drove home had vanished after taking some food, not much because she did not feel hungry; she was content with the bowl of half-eaten salad wilting beside her elbow. In front of her was the file of printouts and articles she had put together on Rosario Cota.

Elena gazed out the window but there was nothing to see; the street was shrouded in darkness and fog. As she sat at the desk, thoughts of Rafael swirled in her mind. They were dark and murky, just like the fog—like the expression in his eyes when he expressed regret at having told about the cardboard box incident.

She felt baffled by his unpredictable behavior, at times rude and nasty, at other times coherent and reasonable. However, even if his ways puzzled her, she was certain that she was not frightened by his mood swings. She felt that she was now even more prepared to roll with the foul language and the violence he had inflicted on others. Yet, something else was seriously troubling her.

After some moments of thought Elena recognized that what was really gnawing at her was that her opinion regarding Rosario Cota's guilt was gradually changing. Rafael was so certain of his mother's innocence that it was affecting her, causing her to experience second thoughts and she did not like the feeling. When she first met Rafael she had been sure, beyond a doubt, that Rosario was guilty and that she would pay justly for her heinous crime. And yet, Elena could not deny that she now felt the ground beneath her shifting on this issue and this alarmed her. She thought of Rafael's confidence in seeking out people and the more she thought of this, her conviction of Rosario Cota's guilt weakened.

She sighed, took the bowl, and began to nibble on the salad while she thought. She intended to read again the file page by page to refresh her memory on the details of the case, knowing that it would strengthen her position and certainly clear her mind of the doubt that was creeping into it. She wanted to listen to Rafael with an open mind as he spoke of his life, but to do that she had to be sure of what had happened so many years before.

Elena opened the file to the first article that described the crime, the scene, the detectives, and witnesses. It was difficult for her to reread those terrible details but she forced herself to do it. She turned next to other articles that told more about the crime and even opinions as to who had committed it. There were photographs of Rosario with the three children and other pictures of their father, distraught with grief after the slaughter.

Hours slipped by as Elena read, not really learning anything new but affirming what she had thought all along regarding what happened that night. She took more time reading the police report that described a cut-and-dried case. The mother, it stated, did it in a drunken, jealous frenzy. She had tried to kill herself after the murders but failed. She was found sprawled in a pool of her own blood, a gun lodged in her hand, spent shell casings around her. Inexplicably, Rosario Cota had left the youngest child, Rafael, unharmed. The report went on with more details but its conclusion was that she was guilty of murdering her three children in cold blood.

Elena got up and headed for the bathroom where she splashed water on her face because it felt hot and puffy. The picture of a mother portrayed with her three living children was lodged behind Elena's eyes and no matter how much cold water she put on her face the image would not go away. She returned to her desk and the file.

Questions came to her regarding the police report so she re-read it, this time looking for mention of ballistic tests taken to verify that the shell casings found near Rosario matched the gun found in her hand. Elena was especially interested to see if tests had been taken to confirm powder residue on Rosario's hands. The report, however, said nothing about forensics.

Thinking that what she had was a partial report, she checked the pile for additional pages only to find that what she had in her hand was the full report. She had missed that it was stamped as final and complete. Even though dissatisfied, Elena decided to put her questions aside for the time being, thinking that the answers might come later in her conversations with Rafael.

She moved on to the trial transcript where it became clear that Rosario Cota's attorney had based his defense on two points. First, that she had blacked out and was unable to remember what happened because she was intoxicated with alcohol and drugs. Blood taken from her on that night verified this fact. This posed the possibility that a killer could have come into the house and murdered the children while she was in that stupor.

Secondly, Rosario Cota's attorney submitted that the sweater she was wearing when she was found in that stupor was not hers. She could not explain its origin, much less did she have a recollection of having put it on that night. This was a key defense issue because even though the children's blood was found splattered on that sweater it was plausible that the garment had been put on her while she was passed out.

Elena stopped reading, thinking that these two points should have caused doubt in the jurors' minds. It did not make sense that a woman, known for her caring ways with her children, could morph into a monster even if she were drunk and drugged. A person does not transform into something she is not. As for the sweater, Elena thought it believable that someone else wore the sweater and slipped it on the unconscious Rosario. Could that someone be the real murderer?

Elena rubbed her eyes; they were burning. When she returned to the transcript she searched for answers but found none. It was clear to her that Rosario's defense had not followed through on those crucial points that might have given her case a shot at reasonable doubt. After that the prosecutor had somehow blown away any relevance and Rosario's defense crumbled.

The transcript detailed the last part of the trial: The defendant was found guilty. The jury asked for the death sentence and the judge followed through on that recommendation. Elena did not have to read any more because she knew that after more than twenty years on death row as she waited for the appeals process to wind down, Rosario Cota was now waiting to be executed.

"And that's that!"

Elena mumbled as she turned off the lamp and shuffled toward bed. She flopped into it without doing what she always did: brush her teeth, take one last shot on the toilet. She felt too disgusted, too troubled and edgy, so she told herself that sleep might wipe out the turmoil she was experiencing. Once in bed, however, she tossed and turned, punched the pillow this and that way, turned flat on her belly, then on her right side, and then on her left side. She did this over and again for more than an hour until exasperated when sleep would not come, she clicked on the lamp.

"Shit!"

She sat up with her knees crunched against her chest. There was no use rereading the file, neither was there any use in trying to find more information because she was convinced that she had what was pertinent. Whatever else was out there was repetitious and not new. So, where did that leave her now?

After thinking about this for a long while she turned off the lamp, reminding herself that if she was to be in shape to meet with Rafael the next day she needed to sleep; the answers to her questions would have to wait until later. What was most important, Elena reminded herself, was that her task was to write Rafael's story, not resolve doubts about the crime. She was a journalist, not a detective or a judge or a juror. And that was that!

CHAPTER 8

Elena and Rafael made their way toward their usual place—he looking at her through narrowed eyes and she feeling the effects of sleeplessness. She felt cranky but once in the chair she went through the routine of pulling out the recorder and notepaper. When she was ready she sighed heavily and waited for him to speak.

"You don't look too good."

"Neither do you."

"Your eyes are red."

"I didn't get much sleep. Let's get started."

"Hey! You're in a bitchy mood."

"Rafael, please get to your story. Forget about the color of my eyes and my mood."

"Okay! Okay! Where do I start?"

"You were telling me about how you saw your mother in prison."

"You gotta hear all the scoop real bad, don't you?"

"Only because you said that you'd tell me."

"Yeah! I guess I did. It started when I left the mission and the Brothers. It was tough for me to make up my mind to leave. They told me that I could stay as long as I wanted and that made me think twice about hittin' the streets again. On top of that, I was scared. For the first time in my life I felt okay with them guys and I was real nervous about what was waitin' for me out there."

"Why didn't you stay?"

"I told you that I read up on Rosario's case. I knew all the crap that came off the walls and I was on fire. I couldn't stick around to help a buncha drunks even if I was spooked to hit the street again."

"Did you try to see your mother?"

"Not yet, that came later. The Brothers got me a job in a pet shop washin' dogs and cats. I cleaned cages too. The money wasn't great but it got me a room and food while I sniffed around."

"Sniffed around? What were you looking for?"

"Stuff like addresses, maybe even phone numbers, anythin' to put me in touch with someone who knew what went on that night. I wanted to know more than the crap in newspapers and magazines."

"Did you find anyone?"

"Oh, yeah!"

"How?"

"Little by little. It was tough. I got lonely lotsa times just goin' to work and passin' nights in that tight little room. Sometimes it got so bad that I even started wantin' to go back to the streets but somethin' told me that if I did that it would be the end of the road for me. Hey, you wanna hear what I looked like when I was doin' that?"

Again Rafael took Elena by surprise. It had not occurred to her that he might have changed but she was curious, so she moved forward to look at him up close.

"That wasn't that long ago, was it? Why would you look different?"

"I did. If you think I look like shit now you shoulda seen me when I looked like twenty miles of bad road. I bet you woulda thought that I was some ol' wino. I was skinny like a starved mutt and I smelled like dog crap from washin' 'em all day long. People thought I was a walkin' scarecrow and nobody hardly talked to me. Do you think I look like a scarecrow?"

"No. Rafael, why don't you stop talking about what you look like and get to your story."

"Goddamn! I don't like you this way."

"The machine is running."

"Okay. Okay. You wanna know how I did it. Well, I kept goin'. There was fire inside me, right here behind my ribs and it was so strong that it was with me all the time, day and night. But the whole thing was crazy! That heat watered down when I thought of what would happen to me if I walked away from my stinkin' job and even that crappy room where I slept. I didn't want nobody to know who I was. You're not gonna believe it but I used to read all the stuff I got on Rosario every night, over and over. I didn't think of nothin' 'cept her. Then the day came when I knew I hadda do somethin' even if I was chicken about the whole thing."

"Rafael, you've lost me. What is it that you wanted to do?"

"Goddamn it! How many times do I have to say it? I hadda talk to real people about that night, not just look at piles of paper every night. I wanted to hear people tell me what they saw, what they heard, that they could bet Rosario was innocent."

"Innocent? Rafael, you exasperate me! You're going to get me to start cussing just like you do."

"Why not? Go ahead! Tell me that I'm a motherfucker!"

"No! You're not that!"

"Not what? A motherfucker? Why don't you say it? I want you to say it! Motherfucker! Motherfucker! Motherfucker!"

His voice was loud, angry, growing shrill with each word. Elena felt her heart pounding from exasperation and anxiety but mostly fright. She hated that Rafael was getting the better of her balance and self-confidence. It was as if he were the one in charge and she the lost and damaged patient. She leaned back with closed eyes, trying to pull herself together, but when she opened her eyes she saw Rafael glaring at her, his face pale, eyes wide open, and this rattled her even more.

"I don't want to call you bad names, Rafael. I just want to help you understand that your mother isn't innocent."

"Ain't innocent? Just listen up, will you? Maybe you can start seein' it my way. What do you know anyway? All you know is what you picked up from all them stinkin' asshole papers. Will you listen to me? I'm not a jerk! I know what's what!"

Rafael abruptly stopped shouting as he sat on the edge of the chair, his clenched fists quivering in midair, the veins in his neck bulging. His intensity shocked Elena, but she was more frightened by her gnawing uncertainty regarding Rosario's guilt. In those long moments of Rafael's rage-filled silence, it struck her that maybe, just maybe, he might be right. She admitted that what he was saying was true. It was a fact that all she knew was from dead, printed papers, most of them vague and repetitive, some of them even incomplete. She flopped back in the chair, reluctantly admitting that Rafael might know more than she.

"I'm listening."

"Well now, you have to gimme a second. Hell! You gotta way of gettin' me all fucked up. First you kick me in the balls and then you 'spect me to keep on yappin' like a parrot. You gotta wait a minute. I need time to get my shit together. Man! You almost gave me a heart attack."

Elena and Rafael sat, both rigid and glaring at one another, waiting for time to pass. She knew that she had gone too far, yet she did not regret it because he had opened up even more. Also, a different way of thinking had crept into her.

"Okay, here's what came next. First, I made up my mind where to look for them people. I got names, but then I saw that they all lived up in Salinas, at least that's what I thought for openers. There was one that didn't. The maid who worked in our house when the kids was killed ran for it after that night. Her name is Candelaria Fontes, but she lives down in Mexico. It turned out that she got so spooked that she split and never came back.

"At first I thought that I would just forget about her. Hell! Who wants to go all the way down to Mexico? I guess I was chicken, but after a while I started gettin' all revved up thinkin' that I would travel down to talk to her. Why not? I knew that I could buy a cheap bus ticket down to the border and from there I could make it to where she was livin'. Then one day, after thinkin' it over, I made up a backpack, stashed my other stuff in a locker at the station, and jumped on a bus headin' for Mexico."

"Wait a minute, Rafael. How did you know where to find this woman?"

"Abuela talked a lot about her and I remembered. I even remembered the name of her town, a place called Etzatlan. Have you ever been in Mexico?"

"Once for a vacation."

"Where?'

"Mazatlan."

"I remember that place. The bus I was on made a stop there. Anyway, I was real jittery about goin' down there, 'specially 'cause I couldn't speak hardly no Spanish. Just about all I know are dirty words that I picked up in the barrio. The good ones that Abuela taught me went away a long time ago. I was so scared that I wouldn't be able to talk to Candelaria that I almost made a U-turn, but then I thought that if I spooked so easy, how could I follow through with the other people? I might as well pack it all in, right? So I made up my mind and hit the road from L.A. to Tijuana, then all the way to Etzatlan."

"Did you have her address?"

"No."

"How did you expect to find her?"

"The place is a little town. There was no way I wouldn't find her and I did."

"That was gutsy of you."

"What else could I do? I needed to start somewhere. It was a long trip and I didn't get much sleep or food, but what does anybody 'spect anyway. I kept my ears open tryin' to pick up on how people talked and you know what? I found out that I talked Spanish a lot, makin' me think that maybe Abuela's talk was still in my head.

"The hours on the road was good for me. It gave me time to think and remember when I was a kid and how much I loved bein' with Abuela. I thought a lot about the kids and about me, that I was alive and that I couldn't understand why. I thoughta my time on the barrio streets, how I passed out all over the place and the voices that clogged up the insides of my head. I thoughta Rosario, caged up for somethin' she didn't do. I thought so hard about her that I could see her face, feel her hands on my face. I felt this even though I never seen her, not even heard her voice. Still, she was there with me on the bus. Both of us was headed south to meet with Candelaria Fontes, to hear the real scoop about what happened that night."

"What about the voices? Did they go away?"

"Hey! There you go again, jumpin' the gun. I'll tell you everythin', but you gotta wait."

Rafael looked at Elena through slanted eyes, waiting for her to react but she did not. She only looked at him, a smile pasted on her face. She raised her hand and pointed a finger at the recorder, prompting him to go on speaking.

"When I got to the station in Guadalajara I felt weird. Everythin' is real different down there and so are the people. I was glad for this brown skin that covers my mug, but I knew that even with that I still looked like a freak. A lotta them dudes took their time eyeballin' me, remindin' me that I was on their turf and that they was the real *chingones*."

"You really picked up on the native dirt, didn't you?"

"Right on, momma! Do you know what a *chingón* is?"

"I know."

"Well, if it's a motherfucker you're lookin' for, a real *chingón*, that's me. Anyway, I sat on a bench lookin' around till I started feelin' okay about bein' there. I looked at a big board that showed a list of towns and buses leavin' that station and there it was. Etzatlan! Just like I knew it would. So I went to the little window and even if I sounded like a moron, I got a ticket. The next thing I knew I was on a bus that was burning rubber, headin' straight to Candelaria Fontes.

"It wasn't no piece of cake when I got off the bus. I picked up smells of fruit and car smoke but my nose couldn't tell no difference between this smell and that other one. When I crossed a street I hadda watch my ass. Them drivers don't give a shit about anyone out in the middle, so I dodged and jumped like a wild burro. There was noise and shoutin' and honkin' smashin' my ears and there was dudes selling crap all over the place. It didn't take me too long to catch on that when I got hungry all I hadda do was go to a stand and fill up. In a way I liked it, but not always. I felt like a goddamn weirdo.

"I found a little fleabag hotel in front of the bus station where the guy at the desk looked at me like I got two heads, but he rented me a room anyway. When I got to it I caved in on the bed right away and I didn't even remember that I was starvin'. Just before I fell asleep I thought that by this time tomorrow I would be talkin' to Candelaria Fontes. Maybe."

Elena glanced at her watch and saw that it was past the time she and Rafael usually broke for the day, but she was anxious to know about his meeting with Candelaria Fontes. This part of his story had not figured into Elena's original plan but now that he was coming up with the information, she admitted that she did not want to wait until later.

"I felt out of it, but not for long. In a couple of days I found out at the drugstore where I could find Candelaria. It's weird, but when the guy behind the jugs and pills told me where she lived I got real scared. I couldn't believe that it was happenin'. I know! I know! Why was I all fucked up if that's what I went there to find in the first place? Right? Well, I didn't think I would get that far, that's why. My guts started to jump all over the place just thinkin' that I'd be standin' eyeball to eyeball with someone who remembered that ugly night. I was so spooked that I started to think that there was still time to make a break for it. After all, Candelaria didn't know I was there, so I could just get the hell outta there and call it quits. Right? Wrong! I stayed and went on the hunt for Candelaria Fontes.

"The pill-pusher took me out to the sidewalk and pointed to where I should go. Just a few blocks down the main drag, he said, then around a corner and up a steep hill to a brown house. The guy told me what it looked like and for sure there it was. I knocked on the door and then I heard a spooky voice tellin' me to come in.

"Hey! I need a smoke! You sure you don't have somethin' stashed away in that big bag of yours?"

Elena did not like the sudden interruption in Rafael's story but she knew why he was doing it. By now she had caught on to his pattern of slamming on the breaks whenever he was getting near anything that made him uncomfortable. She knew it was his way of stalling.

"No. I told you that I don't smoke but I'll tell you what. If you want we can break until tomorrow when we'll both be rested. We've gone longer today."

"You're gettin' bitchy, ain't you?"

"Don't insult me just because you feel rotten about what you're remembering. You're doing this because you want to, okay?"

"I need a smoke!"

"Well, I don't have one and I'm out of here. I don't mind admitting that I'm tired."

"All right, already! I'll tell you about Candelaria tomorrow. I guess you gotta hot date with your boyfriend and you don't wanna fess up."

"No! I'm just tired. Is that okay with you?"

"Don't you have a boyfriend?"

"Do you think I should be telling you all about my private life?"

"Why not? I'm spillin' out my guts to you. All I wanna know is if you have a guy."

"I don't have a boyfriend."

"No? Why are the guys around you so fucked up?"

"I don't know. I'll let you know when I find out."

CHAPTER 9

"I walked into that house. The door was open and I was so stupid that I didn't stop to think that some sonofabitch could sneak up and crack my head open with a tire wrench or somethin' worse. I stood lookin' around like I was a moron, my head twistin' all over the place. I took it all in. The place was big, not like my ol' man's castle but a different kinda big. Then I heard a voice callin' me.

¡Ven!

"I walked to the voice so fast I could hear my footsteps bouncin' off the big ceiling. I slid by plants and even a fountain in the middle of the place. I ain't never seen nothin' like it but it looked cool, with flowers stickin' out all over the place. I liked the bubblin' noises coming from the water.

¡Ven!

"There it was again and the word kept soundin' over and over till I found the room where it was comin' from. It was dark, but when my eyeballs cleared up I made out a female sittin' by a little table. Still, it was so black that I could only see her back. She was lookin' in the other direction but I knew right off that it was Candelaria Fontes and I moved closer till I could see her up front. I was right. It was the maid who was with my family when the crime happened. She looked at me and I looked at her, eyeball to eyeball. What do you think of that? I landed her all by myself."

"Wait a minute, Rafael. How did you know it was the maid? Had you seen a picture of her? Maybe you picked up a description of what she looks like?"

"Christ! How come you never believe none of the things I tell you? No, I didn't have nobody tell me what she looked like and I already tol' you that she split right after the crime, so how in the hell was I supposed to get my hands on a picture of her?"

"You just knew it was Candelaria Fontes?"

"That's right! You gotta problem with that?"

"No, Rafael. Just go on."

Siéntate.

"She talked in Spanish but I understood. Goddamn! I understood! So I looked around and got a little stool, moved it real close to her, and sat where I could almost touch her knees. Like I said, the place was real dark but there was light comin' in through the long windows. When I looked through 'em I saw a buncha plants and a lotta cages with little birds. Then I turned and took a real hard look at Candelaria's face.

"I 'spected her to be a real ol' bag, maybe with a couple of teeth missin' and her hair all stringy and bundled up in a bun, but I was wrong. She ain't that ol', maybe just a few years older than you. Candelaria is all *india*. Her skin is real brown and smooth, her eyes gray or maybe even green. Her hair is thick and black mixed in with a little bit of silver and it was pulled back in a fat braid. She was dressed like a Valley girl, not like a *mamacita* but like a worker. She was wearin' sneakers, jeans, and a cowboy shirt. On top of it all she wore a *rebozo* coverin' her shoulders.

¿Eres Rafael Cota?

"She sat there, all bug-eyed, just starin' at me. She looked and looked at me from the top of my head down to my feet, then back up to my face. She probably couldn't understand who the ugly slob sittin' in front of her was. After a while I started to get nervous 'cause she didn't say nothin' more.

Sí.

Lo sé. Te pareces a tu mamá.

"You look like your mamá! Goddamn! Her words made my belly kick up somethin' awful 'cause I remembered that's what Abuela always said. My brain got all messed up just thinkin' that here was somebody who had taken me in her arms when I was still too little to walk and that she was with my family when they was alive. Thinkin' that way made me shake like a wet mutt and I knew that sweat was poppin' up all over my face. I tried to look cool but I knew that she knew that I was messin' up.

I will speak English even if it is stiff.

"Candelaria looked at me with slanty eyes, kinda nervous and careful, but her voice was good. I liked it. I could tell that she didn't know what to make of me but was gonna talk to me anyway, even if she saw that I was a big-time asshole. That was okay. I didn't care what she thought of me as long as she came across with what I wanted to know.

I am sitting because I hurt my knee.

That's cool. I mean, it's good to sit here with you.

"After that we kept quiet. I didn't know what to say even if I knew it was up to me to open up. I was so messed up I just didn't know what to do. Should I just come out with it and ask her if she knew who whacked my sisters and brother? But nothin' came outta my trap no matter how much I tried. Christ! Why did I turn out so stupid? No wonder the ol' man hated me.

Stop being afraid.

"God! She seen the sweat runnin' down my ugly face and she knew that all the shakin' meant that I was fallin' apart. She even knew that I was close to passin' out when she asked me about Rosario.

What about your mamá?

She's in prison.

Still? I heard that she was condemned to die but that was a long time ago.

Sí. In California it takes a long time to make things like that happen.

¡Ay, esos gringos! Poor woman. Locked up all these years. Maybe she will be set free. What do you think?

Maybe. I mean, I hope so. That's why I'm here.

Do you visit her often?

I'm waitin' for permission to see her.

Permission? Why? You are her son.

I still gotta wait.

Have you seen her before?

No.

Why not?

I tried but she didn't wanna see me.

"Candelaria stayed real quiet but I had the feeling that she knew why Rosario didn't wanna see me. I almost asked her but I didn't have the goddamn nerve.

And your abuela?

She died a long time ago.

"She looked up at me and put her hands together like she was prayin'. She sat there, all the time eyeballin' me, lookin' through me like I was a rag or somethin', but I couldn't tell what she was thinkin'.

And your papá?

I ain't seen him in a long time.

You do not live with him?

No, he threw me outta his house. I live here and there, any place I can get a job.

In California?

Yeah. In L.A., far away from where we lived when you was there.

How do you make a living?

Doin' this and that. Sometimes I work in grocery stores or gardenin', mosta the time washin' and combin' dogs.

"All that crap I was tellin' her was true but I didn't tell her about my barrio days, or the pool halls and liquor stores. And there wasn't no way I was gonna tell Candelaria how I messed up on the streets, but her eyes cut into me like she was readin' my heart. I knew that she knew.

Rafael, you should be a lawyer or a doctor or someone powerful.

Like my ol' man?

"I knew that this part hit her real hard. She turned away like she didn't want me to see into her eyes. Then I started gettin' scared that she was gonna clam up on me, so I beat her to it.

Tell me about 'em.

Your brother and sisters?

Yeah.

They were like most children. They played. They were traviesos. How do you say this in English?

I don't know. Maybe twerps?

Yes, that's it, but in a good way. Rudy, the oldest, was always playing jokes. The three of them liked games.

How was they at home?

What do you mean?

Did they laugh and talk? What was it like in the house?

Happy. Except when your papá and mamá fought. Then the children got sad, especially Rudy. I think it was because he was old enough to understand how terrible it was.

What was the fights about?

Ugly things. Cruel things.

Tell me about that night.

Why? It's the past.

Not for me.

I think you want me to tell you who committed the murders.

Yeah.

I do not want to talk about it, Rafael.

Please talk to me.

Let the dead rest in peace.

Rosario ain't dead yet.

I do not know who did it. All I know is that it was not your mamá.

How come you say this? Did you see who did it?

No. All I know is that she did not kill the children but I do not know why I say this. Perhaps it is because she was a very good mother. She was loving with the children. No, it was not possible for her to kill them.

Did you say this to the cops?

No.

Why not?

Because I got scared and ran away.

"I got pissed when Candelaria said this. Honest to God, I wanted to slap her 'cause she ran away instead of stayin' to help Rosario. It woulda made a big difference but she chickened out. I guess she knew what I was feelin', almost like she was seein' what I was thinkin'. She even tried to tell me why she had spooked so bad.

The reason for my silence is not easy to explain or for you to understand. It is complicated, filled with dark corners and twists. Part of my silence came from fear, not only for myself, but dread that telling what my eyes and ears witnessed might unleash even greater demonios.

In the beginning, when I ran away, I thought that one day I would forget what I had witnessed in that house of misery. I was convinced that by returning to my native land where I could speak in my own tongue, by living as if I had never entered that world of hatred, I would forget the calamity. But now I know that I was wrong because pictures of three small dead bodies are engraved on my heart and frequently disturb my sleep. Now, I regret that I ran away.

When it was time for me to leave the house that night I heard fighting coming from the kitchen. Your mamá and papá often had terrible arguments but this one sounded more enraged than most times, so I walked quietly and stood where I could not be seen. Such words, such hate! They were drunk. I knew it. Then unexpectedly Rudy was standing by my side, shaking and shivering like a little bird. He said that he was going to call the police but I stopped him. I told him to go back to bed. He did.

Soon after your father rushed out of the house and then I heard his car speed away. I stayed where I was hidden and I saw your mother go upstairs. I remained hidden for a long time until I heard the car return and he rushed into the house and up the stairs. Then the explosions happened.

Who did it, Candelaria?

I do not know. All I know is that it could not have been your papá, much less your mamá.

How do you know it wasn't him?

I just know.

You musta seen somethin'! Somebody!

No! I am telling you the truth! I only saw what I have just told you.

Who did it, Candelaria? Are you coverin' somebody's ass?

No! I am not protecting anyone.

Then who did it?

Perhaps it was an intruder.

Intruder? Why? What for?

I do not know! I do not know! What I do know is that I ran out of the house until I reached my brother's house. Miles seemed like nothing to my poor legs because fear filled me with indescribable strength. When I ran through the door, my family thought that I was demented and it was a long time before I could speak even though they rubbed my arms and forehead with alcohol. I never told anyone what I have told you. Not the police, not the judge.

Candelaria, do you believe Rosario is innocent?

Yes.

Will you come with me to say this to the cops?

The police?

"It was right there that she slammed on the brakes. I shoulda seen it when she got real quiet and her skin went green. Now when I think of it I can't blame her. I mean, there she was lookin' at a loser like me, asking her to walk into the hands of the law to talk about somethin' that happened twenty years ago. Who can blame her?

"What can I say? I was a real asshole. I didn't see it clear and I kidded myself into thinkin' that she'd come back with me to save Rosario. Still, I told Candelaria that there was a bus leavin' the next day and would she come with me? I thought she said yes, but now I know that I was jivin' myself. After a while she said that she had a buncha things to do, but I guess she was just tryin' to get rid of me. Anyhow, I told her to meet me at the bus station the next day.

"Next day, like a stupid jerk, I went to the station, bought two tickets, and waited for her but nothin' happened. Goddamn it! Nothin'! I waited and waited. Buses went and came. People went and came but still I waited. I started to sweat when I saw people climbin' on my bus but still no Candelaria. I walked up and down, lookin' and stretchin' my neck, but no Candelaria. When it was time for the bus to leave, the driver slammed shut the door. I went up to his window and asked him to wait but he just looked at me like the dickhead I was and stepped on the gas. I kicked the tire but he was outta there. People, bus, everythin' left me behind smellin' the stinkin' smoke.

"I sat on the curb for a while till the devil got into me, then I got on my feet and ran all the way to Candelaria's house. This time the door was closed tight but no matter how much I banged, nothin' happened. I yelled out her name over and over. Nothin'. Then I kicked at the door hopin' to cave it in but it was a big, heavy goddamn thing and I didn't stand no chance. I bashed on it with my hands till blood started to drip down my sleeves. I screamed till my voice gave out. That's when I felt a cop's nightstick smack me across the back of my head and I dropped, stunned and blurry-eyed. On the way down I seen two cops and I knew it was over. They picked me up and made sure that I made it to the bus station where they put me on the first stinkin' bus north."

Rafael fell silent at this point; his story was over. Elena waited, keeping her questions to herself because she sensed the deep gloom that had come over him. One edgy comment, she knew, might push him even deeper into that dejected mood.

"She double-crossed me."

"Rafael, she didn't say she'd come back with you."

"She chickened out."

"Can you blame her?"

"She didn't have to blow no whistle on me."

"Rafael, you just said that you understood her, that you fooled yourself into believing she'd come back. You have to hang on to that. It was too much to expect of her."

"Too much? This is Rosario's life we're talkin' about, remember?"

"People are unpredictable when they're scared. We're all the same."

"She coulda been a big help to me and Rosario."

"Maybe she wasn't sure of what she said to you."

"Like what?"

"Like about an intruder being the killer."

"That's the only thing that coulda happened. Some creep snuck in through a window or some other place and blew the kids away. He tried it with Rosario but that's when the ol' man broke into the whole thing."

"What would be the motive?"

"Money. The ol' man is rich and everybody in town knows it. Maybe the bastard never thought about murder but at the last minute he lost his nerve."

"Did Candelaria Fontes say Rosario was innocent?"

"Yeah!"

"In those words? Did she actually say, *I believe your mother is innocent?*"

"Not like that, but she said *yes* when I asked her about it."

"Yes to what?"

"Yes to somebody else doin' it."

"I don't know, Rafael."

"What don't you know?"

"I don't know what made Candelaria so sure that it wasn't your mother who killed the kids. How could she know when she really didn't see anyone do the actual killing?"

"Goddamn it! There you go again! Which side are you on anyway?"

"It's not a matter of taking sides, Rafael. I'm just trying to get a handle on what might have happened. As it now stands a jury found your mother guilty. I just want to see if the jury was wrong."

"Well, that buncha dickheads was wrong! Wrong, I tell you! Oh, what the hell! So what if Candelaria chickened out on me! So what if she called the cops on me! It didn't stop me, did it?"

"Did you hear from Candelaria after that?"

"Nope, but who gives a shit? I got better thoughts on the trip back to the States. I didn't need her. I had other ideas."

The tape recorder had shut down a while before and Elena let him know that it was time to quit when she began to pick up her things. Rafael did not move and he looked at her with dejected eyes.

"See you tomorrow."

"Yeah."

CHAPTER 10

Elena drove toward Absalom House that morning with one person on her mind: Candelaria Fontes. She felt saddened that Rafael believed that she would return with him to bear witness to his mother's innocence. That had hurt him deeply, but nothing could be done about it. Maybe it was even understandable since Candelaria was probably not being honest regarding Rosario Cota's innocence. This is what Elena really thought.

On the other hand what if Candelaria was telling the truth? This thought paused Elena's mind because it was easy for her to deal with Rosario's guilt but what about her innocence? That was the nagging question she still could not answer. She pushed back these thoughts as she walked toward Rafael.

"Good morning, Rafael."

"Hi."

"Feeling okay?"

"Yeah."

He was sitting in the usual chair staring out the window. He barely turned to face Elena even when she spoke to him and she knew he was not in a good mood. It would be a hard session but she was determined to follow through on asking more about Candelaria Fontes. Elena set up the recorder and pulled out a notepad.

"Rafael, I've given a lot of thought to what you told me yesterday about Candelaria Fontes."

"Yeah? So, what about it? You wanna go over it again?"

"No, you were clear about the whole thing."

"What else do you wanna know?"

"What impact did it have on you?"

"What?"

"How did it hit you?"

"What do you think? I felt like shit. How would anybody feel after being double-crossed and then dragged to a stinkin' bus by cops? I didn't 'spect Candelaria to sic the cops on me, honest to God!"

"She didn't betray you. She got scared."

"Scared my ass! It was nothin' but a lousy curve ball. If she was scared why didn't she say so? Why not spit it out and not go behind my goddamn back? She acted like my ol' man, sneaky, sayin' one thing and doin' something else. She stabbed me in the back and I hated her for it. I even bawled but nobody on the bus saw the snot runnin' down my mouth and chin 'cause I threw my jacket over my head."

"So you misunderstood her about coming with you, Rafael, but you're forgetting the important part: she said that your mother is innocent."

"No, I didn't forget. After I stopped bein' pissed I started to feel strong. Now I knew for sure that Rosario was innocent. I mean, I always knew it but hearin' Candelaria admit it gave me a big shot of confidence. And there was more. Now I had a pile of stuff on what happened that night and the picture wasn't a big blank no more. That gave me a handle. So, maybe bein' kicked in the ass was worth it.

"What the hell! After a while I said to myself that maybe even I woulda come up with a chicken liver if it came down to facin' a buncha cops and judges. And the more I thought of the trial the more I knew that it was all a pile of horseshit anyway. The real thing was covered up, so what good would it do to drag Candelaria back to take a beatin'? Thinkin' this way helped me get over what she did to me. Anyway, I felt strong that I was on the right track, that I wasn't lookin' for just nothin'.

"While the bus made tracks, little towns passed by the window one by one and I got stronger and stronger. I knew that Rosario didn't snuff my little sisters and brother and I was still gonna prove it, just like Abuela said I would. It hit me again that it was why I was left alive that stinkin' night.

"But something real weird happened to me on that trip. It happened just one time but it was so tough that I almost lost it. The ol' man's face suddenly came up right in front of me. That's right, it showed up outta nothin' and it hung in the dirty air so close to me that his big nose rubbed mine.

"Do you wanna hear about that part? Yeah? Well, the bus was rumblin' and swayin', burnin' rubber like hell but I saw that mug with its smooth round cheeks and its ugly curled hair sticking out like corkscrews. It was so real that I thought the ol' man was right there sittin' in front of me and lookin' at him spooked the crap outta me. He had that ol' look, real grouchy, his mouth all straight and stiff. I could tell that he was yellin' at me even on top of the racket comin' outta the motor.

"I shook my head tryin' to hide from his dirty looks but the thing didn't go away till I rubbed my eyes. After that I forced myself not to think of what happened. I looked out the window hopin' the trees and bushes would help me forget him. It did and the ugly mug didn't show up again. I wasn't thinkin' of nothin' that happened inside or outside the bus after that. All I cared was that I was headin' north back to California, back to L.A. and the Valley. All the while I was fig-urin' out my next step.

"I thought that once in town, gettin' a new job was my next move just so I could support myself while I went back to the piles of papers I had stashed away. I had to read all that stuff again, not once but lots a times and I needed a place to sleep and eat while I did that. I lucked out pretty quick and found a job with a meatpackin' company where I worked from real early in the morning.

"The work wasn't no big deal 'cept that it was so cold in the giant freezers that I had to wear a couple of sweaters and no matter how much I bundled up my ass was always half frozen. But it was okay. The job got me some money and time and I had Saturdays and Sundays to myself. That's when I went to work readin' and figurin' out more names of people I wanted to track down.

"Them was days when I was alone more than ever. It was weird. I was a stranger on streets where I used to cruise, on corners where I hung out but that was all right with me. That's how I wanted it to be. I didn't wanna talk to nobody. It was like I was the only goddamn human being in the barrio, a lone desert coyote howlin' at the moon. Sometimes the naggin' voices came back big time but I took no bad news from 'em and talked right back. I told the noise to get down, to be still, and they did what I ordered.

"You know what? Now when I look through the wired windows of this funny farm, I think that I shoulda stopped right there and maybe even run away. I shoulda known that them voices was tryin' to tell me somethin' but I didn't pay no attention. I guess that things would be different if only I'd stopped messin' with them sleepin' dogs."

"Rafael, did you have a special girlfriend? Someone to date?"

"What kinda question is that? What's it got to do with what I'm sayin'?"

"A friend might have given you company, that's what I mean."

"Well, no. I told you that I did a lotta that stuff when I hung around the streets but not afterward."

"Yet you're letting me understand that you should have left things as they were. Maybe someone special could have helped you."

"You wanna hear my story or about girlfriends?"

Elena sat back in the chair. She was now convinced that Rafael had led a solitary, sad life that had taken him down the path that ended in Absalom House and that even now he was unwilling, or incapable, of seeing that reality.

"Nothin' made me give up. I pushed more, sniffin' out anyone who could remember even a little part of what happened on that night. I didn't stop. I was a pit bull dog, slashin' and tearin'. I made phone calls and wrote letters. I used up all my free time and money lookin', lookin', but I only kept crashin' into a buncha dead-end alleys. People are weird. They change phone numbers and move around like a buncha gypsies.

"Can you believe that I wrote letters? Yeah, me, stupid Rafael! *Dear Miss Neighbor lady. I'm the kid that made it alive! Do you remember my mother? What about my ol' man?* Each time I put one of them letters in the mailbox I got all jacked up thinkin' that for sure I was gonna hit gold. Yeah! But then the thing would be returned marked with a nobody-home stamp. Pretty much the same thing happened with phone numbers that I dug up. Each time I tried one, the thing turned up disconnected or wrong.

"You don't know how pissed I got after doin' this a pile of times and the day came when I almost gave up, but then a break came along! I almost ran outta juice when the number I dialed answered. What do you know? Some ol' bag came on the line and I nearly got a heart attack when she said she remembered my family. I talked real nice and easy tryin' to hide that I was scared that she would hang up on me.

Hello! Hello! Hello! Who is this?

My name is Rafael Cota.

Yes?

Do you remember the Cota family?

Yes. I remember them.

I'm the kid that made it out alive and I wanna know what you remember about that night.

What do you mean?

What do you remember about the crime?

Look, I don't want to be rude but I don't even know who you are or what you really want. The awful thing that happened that night is on the record. Go read about it. That's all I have to say.

Lady, all I wanna know is if you think my mother is guilty.

What kind of question is that? Go find the answer yourself.

That's what I'm tryin' to do! Just gimme anything you know about the kids, about my mother. Anything!

Look, I'll say what I said to the police. Rosario was a good mother and a good neighbor and I think, I've always thought, that it's impossible that she did such a horrible thing.

Lemme visit you.

No!

I need to talk more to you.

No! I have nothing else to say.

"Then, slam! She hung up on me, just like that! I think it was my fault 'cause my voice got real loud and wobbly at the end. I couldn't help it and I guess I spooked the ol' bag. But you know what? I wasn't put down even if she wouldn't see me. All I knew was that she almost said that Rosario was innocent. Can you hear me? That's what counted! I didn't need the ol' bag after that. No way, Jose! It meant that I was on the right track.

"I felt all cranked with what the ol' bag said. I thought and thought about it and I felt pumped like I just beat the shit outta the meanest barrio creep. I wanted to pick up the phone to call Abuela. She was the only one who knew what I was feelin' but she was dead."

Elena watched Rafael as he rocked back and forth on his rump, first rubbing his palms one against the other, then lifting his arms and flexing his biceps, jabbing his fists as if posing for a photograph; an expression of triumph was pasted on his face. For a moment she thought that he was acting like a schoolboy, bragging about this or that, but then she realized that it was his grown-up resilience that was amazing her. She saw that in the end nothing deterred him from his focus, that despite put-downs he was always ready to pick up on whatever crumbs might support his belief in his mother's innocence.

On the other hand, Elena thought if that voice on the other side of the phone had really stood by Rosario's innocence, even if only by suggestion, then he had reason to be encouraged. She again felt a wave of doubt washing over her but she pushed it away.

"My next move was to plug into the chief honcho detective, the dude who investigated the murders. I collected a lotta dope on that guy from newspapers and magazines. His name is Kevin Haas. Ain't that one shitty name? But that's the way it is. I tracked him down and wouldn't you know it, he had moved to live down near me when he retired. Gettin' his phone number was easy.

"All I did was call his ol' station and even when they gave me the runaround about not givin' out information, I got the chick on the other end of the phone to take my number at work so that the dickhead could call me. How did I know that he'd come across? Easy! All I said was that I was the kid who wasn't murdered in the Cota killings and bam! I got a call from him the next day just when I was packin' my last box of sausages.

"At first the guy was real cagey, askin' questions like who I was and how I got his number. I tried to sound like he didn't spook me, but, honest to God, I was so uptight that I was shakin' all over, right down to my ass. What helped me out was that I could hear him breathin' real hard, so I knew that he was feelin' pretty chicken himself. When he finally asked me what I wanted to know, I worked up the guts to tell him that I couldn't talk over the phone, that I wanted to meet him in person. Was that goin' over the edge, or what? After I said that he clammed up and I thought he hung up on me but no, he was still there. Then he gave me a little test.

How old are you?
Twenty-three.
What's your father's name?
Joel Cota.
What was your mother's name?
Rosario Cota.
Didn't she commit suicide soon after the murders?

No. She's in Quentin waitin' to be fried.

"That did it! I knew that I passed his little test and I caught on that he was even more spooked than me when I heard him gulp back a goober. Then he told me to meet him the next day at a place called Point Fermin, right on the beach down there.

"After work I picked up a pizza and went to my room where I pulled out all the crap I had on the Haas Man. I sat for hours readin' the stuff till my eyeballs almost fell out. I found a couple of pictures that I put under my little lamp and looked at 'em till I nearly made them burn up.

"The Haas Man has a weird face that jumped outta the pictures and the more I looked at that mug the bigger it got, just like Frankenstein's, hard and square. Just lookin' at the pictures I could tell from the face that the dick was spooked outta his gourd the night of the crime. For sure he was really feelin' shitty.

"My belly was in a big knot so I forgot all about the pizza. I knew that I was gonna mcct with the guy the next day and I was scared at what he would say about Rosario. I flopped on the bed without even takin' off my clothes, without even drinking a glass of water. I knew that I was gonna fall asleep but I fought it off thinkin' what if the stinkin' nightmare came back to me? What if the shadow that murdered the kids squeezed in from under the door and pointed the goddamn gun at me? After a while, I couldn't help it and a black cloud swallowed me up.

"Next day I sat waiting on a bench for the big dick. It was by a Chink bell high on a cliff but he wasn't there so I sat lookin' around like a moron. From there I could make out the ocean and people down on lawns barbequin'. I looked to one side and made out the cliffs with a lighthouse; to the other side was a big park.

"He snuck up on me all of a sudden and when he talked he scared the crap outta me. This time his voice wasn't shaky and it shook me up bad while he stood lookin' down on me like a goddamn bouncer with his legs spread open. I didn't answer him 'cause I didn't know what the hell to say, so he sat next to me, all the time eyeballin' me. I acted like I was feelin' real cool and looked out to the ocean till I finally got the guts to open up.

Rosario is gonna fry pretty soon.

I know. What's that got to do with me?

Nothin', I guess.

Then what's this all about?

What about that night? You know more than what's in the newspapers.

What makes you think I know more?

I'm just hopin'.

Hoping? For what?

I'm hopin' that you tell me somethin' new, somethin' that you remember about that night.

"The guy was about seventy years ol' but in pretty good shape. He was real quiet, eyeballin' me till his eyes almost fell outta his mug and pretty soon them boiled-fish blue eyes started to make me feel like shit, but I made myself stop the shakes that was takin' over me. I had more to ask him and couldn't waste time lettin' myself turn chicken. I stared back at him, givin' him my ol' Indio slant-eye look and in a few minutes he cracked and started talkin'.

You're the baby that made it through?

Yeah. I'm Rafael.

Okay. What do you want to know?

I don't believe Rosario did it.

"When I said this the dick acted like I kicked him in the balls. He licked his flabby lips, started squirmin' around on the bench but then all of a sudden he stopped movin' and stared at me real hard.

Look, kid, forget it. I'm going to be blunt with you and come right out and say that I have no doubt that your mother killed those three kids. You'd better stop wasting your time and eating your heart out. You've got to accept it. That's all there is to it.

Fuck you! What makes you so sure?

Hey! Don't get cute with me. Watch that mouth! Remember who's doing who the favor here.

Sorry.

Okay. We were sure because we checked out every shred of evidence. We went over the crime scene hoping to find something that would tell us that it was an intruder that had committed that god-awful act. We worked days, nights, tons of hours, but in the end the evidence against your mother was overwhelming and undeniable.

Like what?

Like her bloodied palm prints on the wall of one of the bedrooms.

That's a crock! Rosario was doped up and unconscious. The real killer coulda dragged her, put her hand in the blood, and plastered it on the wall. Besides, did you ever test the blood to see who it belonged to?

We didn't need to do it. It was obvious that the blood belonged to one of the kids, maybe to all three of them. Besides, if she had been dragged, there would've been tracks on the rug, some sign of that happening. It isn't easy to drag an unconscious person from one place to the other without leaving at least some traces.

My ol' man coulda picked her up and carried her to the room.

Your old man? Are you saying you think your father did it?

I'm not the only one who thinks that way.

Look, I know how you feel. I don't know what I would be going through if my ma was about to be fried. But like I already said, the evidence was too much and too hard to deny.

Like what?

You want more? Okay! Like there were pieces of brains splattered all over your mother's sweater. There was skin embedded under her fingernails that was scratched off the kids' faces and necks.

Did you skip testin' all that crap just like you skipped the other things?

I'm warning you. Don't get snotty with me. We knew what we were doing.

When your guys found Rosario, she was passed out on the floor in the bedroom. Right?

Yes.

She was bleedin', right?

Yes.

There was bullet casings scattered around her. Right?

Yes.

The rod was on a dresser, a few feet away from her. Right?

Yes.

Well, how did you explain that happenin'? How could she empty the casings from the gun after she shot herself, put it on a dresser, then drop where you found her?

Look, Rafael, don't you think we questioned this? Don't you think this came out in the trial? When your father came back from his office, he went to the bedroom and found her on the floor, moaning and mumbling. He picked her up and found the gun under her. Without thinking, he grabbed the gun, spun open the cylinder, and the casings fell out. Before he knew what he was doing, he put the gun on the dresser, reached for the phone, and called the police. As he did this, he still had no idea what had happened to your brother and sisters. It wasn't until the dispatcher asked if there were any kids in the house that he ran to the bedrooms and found the horrible scene.

Was his fingerprints on the piece?

We didn't check. There wasn't any need to do that.

What about the maid?

Yeah? What about her?

Did you get her story?

No. She disappeared. She hit the road back to Mexico.

Was there anythin' you guys really checked out about the whole mess?

I already told you, don't push me around or I'm out of here!

"I felt so goddamn pissed with the guy that I couldn't talk no more. What I was hearin' was uglier than all my nightmares put together. I could feel my ol' man shakin' my shoulders like when I was a brat, I could hear him sayin' that my neck was gonna get stretched a mile long. What the dick was sayin' was worse than when I was a zombie on the streets of L.A. I just sat on that goddamn bench thinkin' that Rosario had been framed and there wasn't nobody besides me that was tryin' to help her. I was sinkin' fast when the guy spoke up.

Rafael, what do you think happened?

You wanna know? Okay. I think my ol' man gave Rosario some shit in a drink so she passed out. Then when he came back home he plugged the kids. After that he went to the bedroom where she was all blacked out and he shot her. Only he messed up and didn't kill her. Then he tried to cover up by wipin' the prints off the gun, carryin' her over to the bedroom where he smeared blood on her clothes, and plastered her fingerprints on the wall. That's what I think.

There are holes in what you're saying but let's say that it's all true. What would have been his motive?

He didn't love her no more.

Oh, I agree on that one. Your father didn't love your mother but as it turned out that was her motive for killing the kids. She couldn't face life without him so she decided to punish him in the worst way. You'll have to come up with another explanation for your father being the guilty one.

I don't believe it! She didn't do it!

Rafael, I understand that you believe in her innocence. The only thing that I've never understood is why you escaped her fury."

CHAPTER 11

The detective got it right. Why wasn't Rafael murdered that night? Why did he escape? Did Rosario Cota hatch some sort of plan or was the answer less complex? Was she interrupted in the act of murdering the other children, forcing her to leave the baby untouched? Or, trapped in hysteria, did she forget about him?

Thinking, Elena sat in the easy chair facing the television set even though it was not on; the screen was blank. She stared at it as if the answers to her questions might appear, giving her a clue to what happened that night. She shared the question regarding Rafael's survival with the detective but there was yet another consideration: Rafael was now accusing his father. This led Elena to ask what happened to Rafael's intruder theory.

To give herself a broader perspective, Elena put aside Rosario as the culprit and began to craft a scenario showing an intruder sneaking into the home that night. The motive? Rafael had credibly given it when he said that money was the reason for the break-in. Why not? Thieves did not need a bigger reason than money to pull off crimes. Yes, it made a lot of sense to Elena but why had the police not come to the same conclusion? Why had they been in such a hurry to pin the killings on Rosario Cota?

Regarding his father's implication, not only did Rafael's version, as he gave it to the detective, hang together but Elena's careful scrutiny of the documents also corroborated that the police buttoned up the case without much testing or questioning. So did Rafael have reason to suspect his father?

She sighed and rubbed her face, afraid that she was in over her head. What had begun as a cut-and-dried writing project had now sucked her in emotionally and she was uncomfortable with the feelings flooding her as she reflected on her encounters with Rafael. Sometimes she felt confident that he was in another world, deluded into believing that his mother was innocent, but at other times Elena felt uneasy and no longer that certain of Rafael's mixed-up notions. Now the question as to why Rafael survived had raised its head, unsettling her nerves, and instead of finding clarity she was swirling with doubts and questions.

Thinking that doing something specific might steady her, Elena went to the desk, opened the laptop, and keyed in the new document that would become Rafael's story. She told herself that a simple outline might focus her mind and put her on the path to writing an objective report. First on the list was Rafael's childhood torn between bitter feelings toward his father and beautiful, lyrical memories of his grandmother. Next, Elena would write about his adolescence on the streets when he turned delinquent and rebelled against school and teachers. After that she would develop what he had said about hearing voices.

As Elena added this to the outline, she stopped suddenly because she sensed that she was about to launch onto the wrong path. If she went in that direction, she would have to include the dreams he was so insistent on retelling and how would she handle that part? Would she insert those hard-to-believe narratives into her writing? After that, how would she deal with the unpredictable shifts in Rafael's moods? What about the foul language and the disgusting behavior he spoke about in such a matter-of-fact way? Would she include these details or leave it to her readers to understand the nature of a twenty-four-year-old man who survived the streets?

Elena's head was beginning to ache again and she admitted that she was stumped, so she moved away from the desk leaving the outline unfinished. After all, there was still so much that she had to know. She needed to hear about the other people Rafael pursued in his obsession to prove Rosario innocent and, most importantly, whatever Elena wrote would have to include the meeting with his mother in prison. After that, the conclusion of her article should deal with the circumstances of his landing in Absalom House. She had understood from the beginning that Rafael had experienced a breakdown, so a description of this part of his life was indispensable to the main point of what she wanted to write.

As much as she wanted to think that she was finished, Elena had to admit that she was not ready to write yet. She would pursue these questions with Rafael tomorrow.

CHAPTER 12

"Rafael, did you mean it when you told the detective that your father murdered the children?"

"Yeah."

"Do you still believe it?"

"Yeah."

"What about the intruder?"

"What about it?"

"It's got to be one or the other."

"Why?"

"Because it can't be both."

"It was a slimebag intruder."

"Not your father?"

"Goddamn it! Why are you tryin' to pin me against a wall?"

"That's not what I'm trying to do. I'm just trying to get a handle on it."

"It wasn't Rosario. That's the only thing you gotta know."

Elena watched Rafael closely as he hunched back, arms folded over his chest, looking withdrawn and morose. She looked out the window wondering about her next step. She decided to go on without asking other questions that might provoke him.

"Okay. After you met with the detective, what did you do?"

"You think I'm real messed up, don't you? Well, maybe sometimes I get things mixed up but I know that Rosario ain't guilty and nobody, not that jerk Haas or nobody else could ever change my mind. It don't make no difference to me what nobody thinks. Not even you."

Rafael fell silent but his chest was heaving. He glared at Elena through slanted eyes obviously meant to intimidate her, but the hard look only pushed her to want more of his story, so she did not react to his words.

"After I left the big dick that day, I took the bus back to the Valley, thinkin' all the way about what he said but there was no way I believed him. Things started to get all mixed up in my head, things like what Candelaria said and the crap the dick came out with. Blah! Blah! Blah! Then on top of it, them voices kept weaselin' into my brain so goddamn loud that I couldn't think straight. The buildings and people outside the bus got all jumbled up, makin' me close my eyes. I knew I looked like some asshole drunk but I didn't care.

"Then my head started to clear up. Candelaria said that Rosario couldn't of done it and the neighbor lady said almost the same thing, so fuck the detective! Right? He was nothin' but a goddamn degenerate anyway, so why even worry about what he said. He might as well put his head down the toilet for all I cared, so by the time I got off the bus I knew I wasn't gonna give up.

"I went back to my room and started diggin' again. I remembered that somewhere in that pile of stinkin' papers I seen that Rosario hit religion once she was put away and that all of a sudden she started hangin' with holy rollers. Abuela used to call 'em *aleluyos*. You know, them stupid assholes that pound a Bible and 'spect a miracle to happen. Well, Rosario hitched up with 'em. At first I didn't pay no attention to all that crap, but after meetin' with the Haas Man I knew it was time to find somethin' different, maybe find one of them *aleluyos* who got in tight with Rosario.

"Then I dug out the piece that talked about a buncha Jesus freaks that got together once a week to pray for Rosario. There it was, right in front of me, pictures showin' a buncha assholes standin' on a street corner, holdin' candles and singin' Okie songs, thinkin' it would spring Rosario from the pen. Whata crock! They might as well be 'spectin' the bunny rabbit to hop along and open up them jailhouse bars.

"The report had a picture of her, too. Jesus! Just thinkin' about it still makes me wanna bawl like a little punk. Rosario was beautiful. She had long, black hair and her smile was like some angel. Her eyes was stars and lookin' at the picture made me wanna have her sittin' right there with me. I wanted her arms around me, squeezin' me, holdin' me real tight. I even started to think that I was a little kid again and I tried hard to remember just one time when I was real tight and close in her arms. I wanted to smell her skin, maybe even feel her cheeks on my face."

Elena looked closely at Rafael, drawn by the tenderness that had crept into his voice, making it fall to a near whisper. His eyes were half closed and there was a childlike smile dancing on his lips. She kept still, not wanting to dispel the mood that had come over him, making her think that perhaps one day Rafael would find peace, even some happiness. Then suddenly his eyes snapped open and his face took on its usual stiffness.

"Well, I let go of that crappy thinkin' pretty quick and looked at another picture that showed the same assholes all over again. There they was, with hard-boiled-egg eyes all corked up into eye sockets, singin' and singin' with a big petition sign propped up in fronta them. *Rosario Cota is innocent!* Man! Did that get me, and instead of likin' 'em, I felt pissed. In a funny way I hated their guts 'cause they was doin' what I wanted to do. Down deep I wanted to kick their ass up their shoulders for takin' my place. I hated that I wasn't in the picture, but then I remembered that I couldn't be there anyway. I was just a little kid when somebody took that picture.

"I wanted to scream, maybe cry, kick the wall, scratch it, and spit all over it. My belly was on fire, but then in the middle of all that, I thought that I had to do somethin' quick before the goddamn voices came back. Did I tell you how they came back and kept buggin' me all the time? No? Well, that's right. I got that company most of the time during those days.

"That night I knew they was there, real close to me, maybe hidin' in the dark or even behind the closet door. The goddamn noisy things would keep quiet for a while but I knew they was ready to escape and start their squawkin', ready to pull their dirty little tricks, always tryin' to drive me bananas if I didn't pull myself together, so I forced myself to read what the paper said.

"That's when I read her name. Sister Gladys Miranda was a nun who did nothin' but help out women jailbirds and, even better, the newspaper said she didn't believe in people bein' fried no matter what they did. Right there! She said it up front! She didn't want Rosario Cota to die 'cause no one's got the right to kill nobody else. Do you hear that? She even used Rosario's name to make sure everybody knew who the hell she was talkin' about. It was the best thing I ever read! That little ol' bag was sayin' just what I was sayin'.

"I kept on readin' like there was fire under my ass when the paper said that Miranda visited Rosario and knew that nobody should snuff her out. How did I miss this newspaper in the first place? How come I didn't see it before? How come I was such a big asshole?

"Right away the next day I started to look up the sister. I couldn't wait to get outta work so I could get to callin' convents and places like that. Where did I start? I got workin' where any moron would start. I looked at police stations in the middle of L.A. and at the female jailhouse. Bingo! I got the Sister's phone number. It's easy to find somebody when you start digging and sniffin' around like a mangy dog and that was me, a starvin' mutt! After I got the number I started to build up my nerve all over again. After a while I called and put on my phoniest con artist voice.

Hello. Can I talk to Sister Miranda?
May I say who's calling?
Yeah. My name is Rafael Cota. Sister Miranda knew my
mother.

"My voice was real smooth and silky. I'm a pretty good con man when I try real hard and I can put on a nifty song-and-dance routine when I wanna. Anyway, the voice on the other end of the phone never asked more, she just said to wait and that's what I did, but my con artist routine got kinda wobbly in the meantime. I started to shake all over, just like when I talked to the Haas Man. I was real glad when Sister Miranda came to the phone and didn't talk too much. All she needed to know was my name but not much more. I guess them sisters work so much with losers they know it's a waste of time to ask a lotta questions since all they get back is a buncha bullshit anyway.

"She said yeah, to come see her on Saturday and she didn't even ask what for. At first I got all crazy and jittery thinkin' that maybe she thought that I was some other bum, or maybe she wasn't even the nun that was in the newspaper I read. Then it got into me that maybe she was so ol' that she was losin' her marbles and she wouldn't know me from any other barrio scumbag. If that happened, where would that leave me? All these crazy ideas started to eat me up till I got hold of the wild horses and told myself that I would go to her house no matter what.

"That Saturday I made it to her place, a convent in East L.A. Jesus! I was a nervous mess! When I made it to the door I stuck up my hand but I couldn't make it knock. I stood there like a goddamn zombie with my paw frozen in the air just like I was Frankenstein or some kinda monster. What if Sister Miranda took one look at me and thought that I was a nut or a dope head, some garbage-can wino off the streets that don't know what he's thinkin'? A pile of years had passed since the murders, why should she remember Rosario or me?

"After a long time I finally got the nerve to knock on the door but nothin' happened. I stretched my ears up in the air till I felt like one of the mutts I used to wash but I still couldn't hear nothin'. Christ! The place was like a tomb but then all of a sudden the goddamn door swung open and it scared the livin' shit right outta me. I hunkered down waitin' for some animal to kick me in the balls but instead a little woman stood lookin' down at me with sweet blue peepers. She was ol' and wrinkled and she smiled at me like she thought that I was a real human being. When I looked up I could tell that she almost laughed at me all hunched over in a ball, just like the roof was gonna cave in on me. I felt like a moron but I straightened up and tried to act normal.

Come in, please. I'm Sister Luke.

Thanks. My name is Rafael Cota. Can I see Sister Miranda?

Yes. She's expecting you. I'll show you to the parlor where you can wait for her.

"I liked her right away. I knew that I looked like a freak but she still acted nice. I walked behind her thinkin' what she thought of my spiked hair and ugly brown mug. All of a sudden I remembered my baggy pants and worn-out sneakers and it hit me that the sister didn't give a damn about my clothes and I liked that a lot, too.

"We walked into a real nice room with a big sofa and pretty things like a big ol' bowl filled with candies. She didn't say nothin' to me, she just pointed to the sofa, then left. I sat down next to a big clock that ticked away like some idiot machine. Then I started eyeballin' the candies and they started to look more and more like they wanted to jump right into my big mouth. It was real quiet in the room 'cept for the tickin' so then I thought what the hell, might as well eat at least one of them little buggers. I peeled one and popped it real quick down my throat. Then I scarfed another one, then even more, but still no one came around. It didn't happen till my trap was filled with chocolate that a voice sounded out almost making me jump right outta my goddamn skin.

Good afternoon.

"All shaky and with my mouth stuffed like a garbage can, I sprang up. I didn't know what to say so I stood there gawkin' at the lady like I was a stupid idiot.

I'm Sister Gladys. Are you the man I spoke to on the phone?

Yeah. I'm Rafael Cota.

"She didn't say nothin' after that. All she did was stare at me like she was tryin' to remember me. Then she came real close to me, lookin' and lookin', from my head down to my ugly sneakers and she did it for a long time, makin' me so nervous that my hands got all clammy.

"Well, I stared right back at her. I didn't want her to catch on to my shakin' guts and while I was at it, I took in her looks. I saw that she was a real ol' lady with hair so white it looked like a wig and her face was covered all over with little wrinkles, just like a dried-out fig but her eyes was nothin' but nice, oh yeah! They was young and bright, just like Abuela's eyes and I liked them right away. Then somethin' made me look down at her feet and I seen that her legs was skinny, just like chicken legs and she was wearin' some big shoes, like she had sores on her toes. But I could tell right away that them chicken legs were ready to stomp all over anythin' that got in her way.

"The problem was that she kept on eyeballin' me till I started to feel like a stupid gorilla that don't know where to put its paws. After a few ticks of the goddamn clock, I decided to let her know that I wasn't no sissy altar boy that would back down just 'cause she was givin' me the evil eye. So I put on my real tough look while I stood with my feet spread out on the floor, just like the Valley homeboys do. I eyeballed her with my Indio slant-eye look till she backed away.

Please sit down. You didn't say what it is that you want of me but I'm here to help with whatever I can.

What do you remember about Rosario Cota?
Cota. Could it be "the" Rosario Cota?
Yeah.
What's she to you?
My mother.
Well, I know she's in prison awaiting execution.
Yeah.
It's been many years.
More than twenty.
Rafael, for a woman my age twenty years is just a sigh. I thought it had been less than twenty years. At any rate, come sit here by my side. I don't bite.

"We sat together on the little sofa but she didn't say nothin' and again she started eyeballin' me. This time her looks was different and I wasn't spooked no more. I even started warmin' up to her, thinkin' that I better watch my garbage-can mouth. I knew she wouldn't like shitty words. Then she patted my hand and smiled. I felt like a punk but at the same time I knew down deep that she was tryin' to tell me somethin', like to relax or chill out.

How about a coke?
No, thanks.

"Crap! Right away, I wanted to kick myself for turnin' down the drink 'cause my mouth felt like sandpaper. I looked at her hopin' she'd ask me again but I saw that she made up her mind to do somethin' else.

Well, Rafael, I would like a cup of tea. Come with me to the kitchen. We can talk while I prepare it.

"I followed her into the kitchen just like I used to do with Abuela, 'cept this one was the biggest kitchens I ever saw. Everythin' was King Kong big. She took me near the monster stove and told me to sit on a stool next to where she was standin'. I remembered that Candelaria Fontes did the same thing. Ain't that weird, I thought.

Sister Miranda, do you know who I am?

Yes. You just told me that you're Rosario Cota's son. And please call me Gladys. Sister Gladys.

Ah, yeah, that's right. Sorry. I'm a little bit nervous.

Don't be.

Thanks. What did you think of Rosario?

What I thought of your mother?

Well, no, not exactly. What I wanna know is if you think that she's guilty.

That's a big, big question. We can talk about it, but first, let me tell you that I feel that I'm standing here looking at a miracle.

A miracle?

Yes. The miracle that you survived, that you've lived to be a grown man; that you're here to ask about your mother.

"You know what? When Sister Gladys said that, I thought of the Haas Man. He said just about the same thing, only in different words. So did Candelaria Fontes. Them words almost caved in my chest, making me crazy. I felt like the Sister put her fingers inside me and she was feelin' all around, touchin' and lookin' for somethin'.

Do you remember me when I was little?

Only in pictures. Your father hid you away from everybody after the death of the children and even more so after the trial. But I can see that you look a lot like your mother, almost identical except that she has fair skin and yours is dark.

"There went the fingers again but I couldn't figure out how anybody could get inside me that way. I was beginnin' to feel messed up when the pot on the stove sprayed out a big noise, making her stop lookin' at me with them little blue eyeballs.

Tell me about her.

Well, I regret to say that I haven't seen her in a number of years so my recollections aren't recent, but my memories of her are still vivid. However, I keep track of her case and I'm heartbroken to know that soon she'll be put to death.

How did you meet her?

I visited her when she was placed in the county jail after her arrest and I saw her every day during the trial. My ministry at the time was to visit the female inmates at that location. I had a heavy load at the time, meaning that there were many women who needed the consolation people like me can sometimes bring. It was there that I met your mother but somehow she stood out from the rest. She was different.

How?

It's hard to explain, especially after so many years. Let me put it like this: There were other prisoners that I still remember. They were rough women, undoubtedly capable of committing terrible crimes. There was one who murdered her husband by burning him in a pit. She first ran over him with a car, then drenched him with gasoline, and finally she torched what was left of him. Poof! The poor man was incinerated in a few minutes. Another woman was a drug addict and a prostitute. She was in prison for beating up a pusher and he managed to live, but just barely. She clubbed him, stomped on him, and even tried to cut off his arms. There was another woman who robbed banks up and down the state. She was there for armed robbery, which is pretty serious business.

I could go on but the point is that Rosario Cota was different despite being arrested for such a monstrous crime. She was refined and very calm. Although she didn't appear grief stricken, at the time I thought, and I still think, that her sorrow was deep in her heart, hidden. In my mind this alone made her different.

Also, she didn't hammer away at her innocence as inmates often do, but she didn't admit committing the crime either. At the time I found her demeanor baffling but after a while that tranquility, that reserve, convinced me more than ever that she should not suffer capital punishment.

Did she finger anybody?

No. She never blamed anyone.

Did she talk about the night the kids was snuffed out?

Yes. Other things, too.

Like what?

I had read in the newspapers that she and your father had had a terrible argument that led up to angry talk of divorce. After many visits, when I felt that she was ready to speak to me I asked her about what I had read. She denied it saying that they had not argued, that they hadn't even exchanged angry words. Instead they had made plans for a family get-together there at their home.

"While Sister Gladys talked I sat on the stool feelin' my brain turn and turn. I was rememberin' what Candelaria Fontes said about the blowout between Rosario and my ol' man. Didn't she say that Rudy got so scared that he almost called the police? But what if Fontes was makin' it all up? Goddamn it! Why did people make up different stories?

They wasn't pissed at each other?

Your mother said that the only thing that upset your father just a little was that the oldest boy, I'm embarrassed but I've forgotten his name, got uppity and kind of sarcastic. In punishment, your father asked the boy to leave the kitchen.

Rudy was his name. That's all that happened?

As I've just said, that's how your mother described that night.

You said there was other things that you talked about.

We talked about God and the Bible. She spoke about you.

Didn't she speak about the kids?

Sometimes, but not as often as she spoke of you.

She didn't talk about losin' the kids?

No.

How come? They was dead and she didn't even cry, or walk around like a zombie? Sister, don't you think that's weird? And what about all the other shit? Didn't you ask her about blackin' out? What about the blood on her clothes and the bloody hand-prints on the walls? Goddamn it! There's gotta be more.

Rafael, watch your vocabulary! Yes, I often wondered about her composure and self-control. I've just told you that it was that very calmness that ultimately convinced me of the evil of putting anyone to death. And, yes, I asked as many questions as came into my mind.

You can't imagine what it's like in a prison. There's only time, plenty of it, and not much else to do but talk. I asked about the blood that was discovered on her clothing and she explained that it had gotten on her because the paramedics had run from the bodies to her trying to save her from dying. Doing that they smeared blood on her.

That hangs together.

Well, some of it does but there's more to it than smeared blood.

What?

The real point was that there was brain matter splattered over her.

So? What's the difference?

Smeared and splattered are different, Rafael. A smear can be transferred from one spot to the other. A splattering happens only once.

Did she say somethin' about clothes that wasn't hers?

No. What difference would that make?

The killer coulda put his bloody sweater on her. That woulda made a difference?

Come to think of it, I remember that came up during the trial. However, she never mentioned it to me.

What else did she say?

She also told me that something was in what she drank and that she blacked out.

I knew it! I tol' the cop that she musta been slipped somethin' that knocked her out.

That's what Rosario often said.

So, did she say she was innocent?

No. She did not. I've already told you that much.

What do you mean? Tellin' you that somebody messed with her brain and that the slimebag changed her clothes says she's innocent.

Maybe. However, she never said, "I'm innocent." That's what I'm saying. Don't you hear the difference?

Okay, Sister, so she never said she was innocent. But there had to be somethin' more than just how she acted that made you go out and get people together to pray and stand around wavin' signs. What was it?

The trial. I was there every day. Believe me, I learned a lot about judges, juries, and lawyers and the ritual that keeps the whole thing going. I watched carefully and pretty soon I began to notice that the judge was not as impartial as he should have been. I mean, I even think he hated your mother.

Every time her lawyer objected, the judge overruled the objection. And every time the prosecutor requested it, there they were, all buzzing and whispering at the judge's desk. Whenever that happened, the result was just about always on the prosecutor's side. More than that, any evidence that might have proved your mother's innocence was rejected; any damning testimony given by a witness was accepted.

That's what convinced me of the injustice that was going on and I organized prayer vigils and demonstrations against the horror of capital punishment. I got people to write the judge to demand that he be fair. This last action really got to him and soon he admonished your mother's lawyer, saying that any further harassment of his court decisions would be held against your mother's case. That did it! We stopped—writing, that is—because we never let up protesting her death sentence.

But something happened after the trial that made me think this whole thing over. It was after the trial, but not too much later, when I got a call from a woman who had been on the jury. She was upset because of the uproar I had caused making people think that Rosario had been unjustly tried. She wanted to let me know that the people on the jury had had a very hard time com-

ing to their verdict. Reaching such a judgment, she told me, was the hardest thing they had ever faced and justice did prevail in the court, regardless of what I thought.

Did you tell her to mind her own business?

No. I said nothing.

Did you ever meet her?

No.

Do you remember her name?

No.

Did she change your mind about what you was doin'?

No, but she made me realize that justice isn't easy. I didn't see her face but I heard the anguish in her voice and I felt deeply for her.

Did you change your mind about Rosario?

No. I still don't believe she should be put to death.

What do you think happened that night?

I think that Rudy saw something—something that spelled out his death sentence—and that of the two girls.

What do you think Rudy saw?

Something.

My ol' man?

"Shit! You shoulda seen Sister freeze right where she was. Then the little cup she was holdin' crashed on the plate and stayed there, welded tight. She didn't blink or breathe or look at me. I said it again but this time I wasn't askin'.

You mean my ol' man!

"Just then Sister Gladys kept her trap shut and all the while I felt my arms and legs gettin' colder and colder, so frozen that I started rubbin' myself all over just like I was naked in the icebox I worked in. Why did I feel that way? Well, I saw that Sister Gladys knew that Rosario was innocent, that she knew somebody else done it.

"My brain started spinnin' just thinkin' of how Rudy musta ran into the killer that night, right when the sonofabitch was doing his thing, maybe even beatin' up on

Rosario. I saw how the slimebag musta caught Rudy eye-ballin' him so he went after the kid. When he whacked Rudy he had to do the same to Rosie and Connie 'cause they saw what was happenin'. Then he tried to snuff out Rosario just to frame her, makin' it look like she pulled the trigger. Jesus! I couldn't help it. The word just slid outta my mouth.

Motherfucker!

Rafael Cota! What did you say? Did I hear you say that horrid, dirty word?

Just mumblin'.

Never say such words again! The Virgin Mary is crying this very minute because she heard what you said.

I'm sorry, Sister, but I'm real pissed. Tell me what you meant when you said that Rudy saw somethin'.

I'll repeat what I said. Everything in me tells me that the child saw something. What that something was, I don't know. So please don't press me anymore on this point.

Do you think it was a scumbag intruder?

Rafael, the only thing that I will affirm with all my strength is that your mother should not be executed. No one has the right to take a human life. That's for God to do. In other words, the day Rosario Cota is put to death she'll join the ranks of the martyrs in Heaven because she will have been inhumanely punished. Now, please, let us end this conversation. I'm very fatigued.

Okay. I'll go now, but I hope you're not all steamed at me. I'm glad that you know what's in my heart. She ain't guilty.

I know, Rafael, and remember that I'll always be here for you. I'm your friend and I want you to call me whenever you need me.

"I walked away from Sister Gladys all messed up. Part of me was glad that she didn't kick my ass outta the convent for the bad language, but another part of me wanted to blow up. What she said about zappin' people only mixed me up real bad. Was she sayin' that Rosario ain't guilty, or was she just sayin' that fryin' people is bad even if they are guilty?

"What about when I wanted Sister Gladys to say somethin' about what Rudy saw? When I tried to push her on it she clammed up real tight. She just wouldn't say it. Why wouldn't she come out and say that it was some slime bucket who broke into the house? And what about my ol' man? She really spooked on that one.

"I went to the bus stop and while I was waitin' I tried to get my shit together. I mean, I had to think about what I got outta Candelaria, the Haas Man, the ol' bag on the telephone, the Sister, and I even threw in the crap from the juror bitch. All that bullshit started to go around in my brain, gettin' all mixed up, makin' my head feel like a goddamn toilet bowl.

"The bus just wouldn't come and I started to feel real crappy. I felt like pukin'. My heart was pumpin' away like crazy. Churnin' in my gut kicked in, gettin' bigger and harder, till I knew that it was the ol' feelin' from my street days when I hated my ol' man more than anythin' else, when I blamed him for the murders.

"Jesus! I felt like I was Plastic Man, one side pullin' against the other one. I was stretchin' in all directions. My mouth filled up with somethin' that tasted like piss and I knew it was hate for the ol' man. It was his fault that this was happenin' to me. I felt like killin' the sonofabitch and make him suffer just like me. I wanted to get a monster needle and shove poison up his ass. I swear I wanted to do that so much that I nearly passed out, right there at the bus stop.

"Then it hit me from behind, like a goddamn bat. Bam! Right on the head! The squeaky voices escaped from somewhere in my sick brain. They slid out yappin', whinin', tellin' me that it was me who was all fucked up, not my ol' man. They shoved me around just like I was some scumbag. Others clicked their long sticky tongues, tellin' me to go ahead and whack the ol' man. They asked what the hell was I waitin' for? They yelled that if I didn't have no balls to do it, why not pull the plug on myself instead? Then, on the other side of Plastic Man came more voices that whispered that I should be ashamed since I was alive and the kids was nothin' but piles of dust at the bottom of coffins.

"When the bus finally came, I got on and made it to a seat. I made out like I was asleep but I was really sluggin' it out with the voices chatterin' and howlin' in my head."

CHAPTER 13

Elena sat looking intently at Rafael. She was stunned into silence by his certainty that his father was the murderer. Rafael's own murderous and suicidal urges also slammed into her with such force that she felt herself shuddering. And what about the voices? She wanted to say something but she did not because she feared that her meaning might miss the mark. Instead she gawked at him, taking a chance that her staring might provoke him to anger.

A whirl of thoughts filled Elena's mind and she drifted off to think about Rosario Cota and the consequences her actions had triggered in Rafael's life; the unspeakable limitations that now imprisoned him. Elena went on staring at Rafael, beginning to understand what he had said: He knew only one way of talking, one way to say what was breaking his heart, one way to react.

Rafael was hunched over, biting his nails, lost in thought. After a few moments Elena pulled her gaze away from him, uncertain whether to continue their conversation or cut it off, but then he suddenly looked at her, his eyes filled with doubt.

"You wanna hear more?"

"Yes."

"I went to the cemetery where the kids are buried. I took a bus and traveled all night and the next morning I got to the place. Why in the hell did I go? Well, the voices poundin' in my brain forced me to do it. They kept yappin' about how that was the only thing I could do for Rosie, Connie, and Rudy.

"Cemeteries are so bad! I hated the place right away. I was lost, but an ol' goat wearin' some ugly cap showed me on a map where the kids was buried, then he pulled me to a path and tol' me to follow it. It was spooky but I started walkin', lookin' at all them slabs of rock with writin' on 'em. It was real quiet. Nothin' was movin' and the only thing I could hear was the wind makin' ugly noises in the trees.

"I walked, lookin' everywhere, but then I started to get a funny feeling, like I was in another country, maybe in some strange place where I didn't belong. Suddenly I stopped and eyeballed the grass, like I could look through it, see people down there under the goddamn mud and I could watch 'em livin' everyday lives, not freaky ones like mine.

"I shook my head when I knew that what I was seein' was weird, that I might be going outta my gourd, so I tried to read the signs that was all over the place just to gimme somethin' else to think about.

He was a wonderful husband and a good provider.
She suffered but is now in Heaven.
He blessed our family with his presence. Our hero.

"Ain't that a crock? I felt all pissed at them signs. I asked how come everybody was so good after they kicked the bucket? I stood there askin' why that writin' didn't tell the truth?

He was a goddamn drunk and wife beater.
She was a hooker that drove us crazy.
Here's a no-good chiseler.

"When I got enough of that stuff, I moved on till I found the spot. I couldn't miss it. It's a big slab of rock carved with the kids' names, when they was born and when they died. I wasn't surprised that it was a monster sign. That's the ol' man, all right! Always showin' off! I bet he paid a ton of bread for that thing.

"Lookin' at that sign was a heartbreaker! All I remember about standin' there is that I wished I could pray, but I couldn't talk to God even when I tried to remember how Abuela prayed. I was dry and didn't know jackshit about that kinda thing. I didn't have the words, so I just sat on the grass and leaned against a tree. It was real gloomy that day and the wind made the tree shake its scrawny branches, makin' me

think it was a skeleton. The place was real lonely and I wanted to bawl just thinkin' that the kids was buried down there,
so alone all them years while I was growin' up, visitin' Abuela,
or jackin' off on the streets of L.A.

"I don't know how long I sat there just thinkin' about my
brother and sisters. I tried to come up with just one little
memory of 'em but all I had was what Abuela tol' me. I
remembered the picture of 'em dressed up in baseball outfits
and I could see their little kid smiles, all filled with big white
teeth. I could even see Rudy's bushy hair stickin' out under
his cap and the girls with braids hangin' down their shoulders.
I saw their round eyes and the way they stood real close. But
that was it. I couldn't remember no more.

"Some kinda crappy feeling grabbed me all of a sudden. I
got to thinkin' that maybe my eyes was right when they saw
people livin' underground. Maybe the kids wasn't piles of
dust after all, maybe they was alive in that other world down
there, talkin', movin', and havin' a good time.

"I looked down at the grass and saw streets with cars and
stores; everythin' was movin'. I could even hear music and
smell good food and—hey! I liked this so much that I let
myself go. I saw the kids all grown up now, older and livin' a
good life under all that mud that was holdin' up my ass.

"Abuela tol' me that Rudy was the builder, that he used
to put things together, all stacked up till it looked like a
house. I thought and thought till I knew that Rudy was a big-
time builder down there, makin' buildings and bridges and all
that kinda crap. Maybe he was even famous all over the world.

"Then Rosie came into my mind and I knew that she
coulda been anythin' she wanted. Anyone that had a pitchin'
arm like hers coulda done anythin', but she was better at
yakkin' so she decided to be a mouthpiece. Ain't that rich?
Abuela said that nothin' could stop Rosie once that mouth of
hers cranked on. Oh, yeah! I saw Rosie the big-time lawyer,

winnin' cases for the mob or other bosses, and everybody loved her just like I loved her.

"I saw little Connie standin' there lookin' at me, askin' what I saw for her, but I tol' her that she was too little to know what she wanted to be when she was whacked. But, you know what? Nobody could know, I told her, 'cause for sure she was somethin' big in her new life. I didn't know! Maybe she was a doctor or a professor, somebody that knows a lot.

"I saw the three of 'em, alive and movin', havin' a helluva time and I loved what I saw. I even felt all that good time suckin' me down close to them, till a shadow came and put the skids on what I was feelin'. All of a sudden I knew like never before that I was alone, that I didn't have nobody to hang with, that I was separated from them. Then I thought that if only I got the chance to live with the kids, we coulda done somethin' special, maybe built things, met people, and even had nice families. I felt so blue 'cause we was locked outta memories we coulda made together, somethin' to look back on when we got to be a buncha ol' goats.

"I knew that some motherfucker had snatched them away from me and we would never do things that would make us laugh our heads off just rememberin'. I felt so sad inside my chest knowin' that I would never be on the same ball team with Rudy or the girls. The more I thought of this, the more I wanted to be in the same picture with 'em, smilin', with a big baseball cap on my head.

"Why did it happen? We coulda been a family, done things, maybe invented new ways to live. Maybe I woulda been a good kid in school, not got in tight with the bums and done all them stupid things. Maybe I coulda been somethin', not the loser asshole I turned out to be.

"I sat on the mud with my head shoved between my knees, feelin' like I was the only scumbag in the whole world. I was alone, by myself, but now I didn't wanna be a lone coyote no more. That only told me that nobody gave a shit about me, that nobody gave a fuck if I stood up or sat down, or jumped, or just rolled over and kicked the bucket.

"Jesus! I knew I was gonna break down and start bawlin' all over the place, but I shut it in, real tight, till I felt that my chest was gonna rip into pieces. Oh, it hurt like hell, but I couldn't let myself cry 'cause I knew that the second I let out the tears the rotten voices would spring into action. How did I know? Oh, I knew they was there, hidin' behind the slabs with all the writin' on 'em. I knew they was waitin' for me to let on that I was losin' my nerve and feelin' sorry for myself.

"I held on tight till my chest just couldn't take it no more. I hadda wail! I hadda open my big trap and let out the pain that was rippin' me to pieces. If I didn't I was gonna blow up. So I cried out like when I was a brat drippin' with pee and scared outta my gourd. I was waitin' for the goddamn gun to blow out my brains.

Hey, Ralphie! You're going real crazy now, ain't you? How deep does a creep like you have to dig before he makes it to China? He-he-he! You got it all wrong, fuckhole! Your brother and sisters are up there in Heaven, not down under your stinking ass. Get it straight! Down there is where you are right now. In Hell where you belong, shithead! Hee-hee-heeeeeeeeee!

"My head snapped around. I wanted to nail at least one of 'em motherfuckers just for once, but I barely caught a quick look at a slimy foot squirmin' behind a bush. I knew that the other ones had made it into hidin' even faster and it was no use going after 'em. *Goddamn you!* I shouted as loud as I could but there was nothin' after that, just the stinkin' tree moanin' in the wind.

"I sat on the mud, pissed and wantin' to kick their ass up their shoulders. I knew they was tryin' to fool me, but I figured that if I sat real still, makin' out like I was cryin', they would creep out again. When they did that I would stomp all over them assholes. But nothin' happened for a long time, so

I gave up and relaxed, but as soon as I did that, there they was again! Them sonsofabitches came out!

Hey, loser! Who do you think you are, anyway? The kids are dead as doornails while you're still alive and kickin'! You, a no-good prick, a shithead flunky, a stupid scumbag! They was gonna be somethin' good, somebody great, not a piece a horseshit like you!

"The goddamn racket got so loud in my head that I jumped to my feet, turnin' around and around like a mutt chasin' its tail, while the voices laughed and snorted. But you know what? For the first time in my life I was fast enough to catch a look at one of 'em. Yeah! I saw a stringy little body with its ugly mug, covered all over with stinkin' brown spots, its ugly trap filled with rotten teeth. Christ! It was so spooky! Its mouth was like a black hole cut into a bald, wrinkled head.

"I screamed like a stuck hog, all the time tryin' to drown out the racket them voices was makin', but they kept gettin' louder and louder, nearly splittin' my head wide open, stabbin' my ears like goddamn spikes, hurtin' like nothin' before hurt me. I spun around, holdin' my ears, tryin' to plug 'em up, all the time trippin', fallin', and rollin' in the mud. I squealed and cried till I heard my voice shuttin' down and I knew that only my big trap was open, but nothin' was comin' outta it.

"I knew what was happenin' to me when my lungs started openin' and shuttin' down like balloons. I knew that I was gonna be sucked into one of my fits. I tried to get up and shake it off, but my heart went off like crazy. The last thing I remember hearin' is the scumbag voices laughin' at me, yellin' out that I was nothin' but a piece of horseshit, a loser, the one that shoulda been whacked instead of the kids.

"When I opened my eyes, the ol' guy with the funny cap was gawkin' down at me, lookin' all worried. His big nose hung more, but I knew it was the same ol' goat that showed me the map.

Are you all right, kid? Should I call 911?

No. Thanks. I fell asleep and I guess I was havin' a nightmare.

"I don't know how the hell I did it but I got up and walked away from the ol' guy, tryin' to look like nothin' was wrong, but when I turned back I saw him checkin' me out like he was sure that I was some weirdo. I looked down at my pants and sweater and saw that they was smeared with grass and mud like I rolled in pig shit. I tried to shake it off but it just stuck.

"I made it to the bus station and tried to calm down while I waited. When I got on, people moved away from me real slow, like nothin' important was happenin', but still they kept on eyeballin' me. I knew they was scared of me. They thought I was a freak but they didn't wanna show they was spooked. I knew what they was thinkin' when they looked at me just like people did when I was a hobo hangin' in doorways and alleys back on the streets of L.A.

"When I got to my room the next day, I felt so bummed that the only thing I could do was fall on the bed where I stayed for I don't know how long with the pillow shoved up against my ears. I was scared of hearin' them voices again. I wanted to croak or to snuff myself out, but I knew that I was nothin' but a stinkin' chicken and didn't have the balls. I shook all over thinkin' that I would have to hear them voices for the rest of my life. I don't remember how long it took but I finally dragged myself to the john when I hadda take a leak. When I peed, the stuff came out limp and puny. Even my piss didn't have no guts.

"I stayed in the toilet for a long time lookin' at myself in the mirror and I scared the hell outta myself. I saw a bony, brown face gawkin' at me, with skin hangin' on to its cheeks just like worn-out leather. My hair was tangled with lumps of mud and grass that looked like horseshit and it was standin' straight up, spiked like I just seen the goddamn devil. I stuck out my tongue and it was covered with white stuff and this scared the hell outta me even more.

"Then I wanted to puke so I got on my knees over the john, but nothin' came outta my guts. I stayed there anyway. I was thinkin'. I was rememberin' how spooked I got in the cemetery, and for the first time in my life I seen that I was scared of a lotta things. Somethin' inside told me that all that feelin' was growin', splittin' and tanglin' inside me, like a buncha snakes.

"I stayed for a long time with my head hangin' over the bowl. I knew there was more inside me that was even scarier than wantin' to kill my ol' man and that was what happened in the cemetery with the scumbag voices. I knew that I came to a road that was real dangerous, that I crossed it into a place where them voices was real. I seen them, and even passed out from being so spooked by them. This scared me more than anythin'. I was afraid that next time I might get trapped on the other side of that road, or maybe I would wanna stay there. Maybe I wouldn't even wanna come back to this motherfucker world.

"I got so shook up that I sprawled on the floor thinkin' that maybe I was losin' my marbles, that maybe even if I heard them voices all my life, this time it was serious. Maybe now I was a real nut and this idea spooked me like nothin' else. I crawled outta the toilet and got into bed without thinkin' of nothin' and I laid there like a stupid dummy.

"I don't know where the idea came from, but after a while I knew that I needed somebody to help me. Abuela's little house on the edge of fields that smelled like fruit and grass slipped into my brain and I wanted to be with her again. I wanted to tell her everythin' that was screwin' me up so bad, let her know that maybe I was goin' crazy and that it was hittin' me all alone with nobody to gimme a hand. Christ! I needed her to be with me.

"Then Sister Gladys showed up in the darkness and somethin' told me that she was the one to pull me outta the hole I was in. I knew she'd listen, that she wouldn't tell me to bug off, that she wouldn't mind my crazy shit. After thinkin' like that, I kicked away all them devils till I finally drifted off to sleep."

CHAPTER 14

Elena Santos listened to Rafael tell of voices and visions and fits of dread. Now she truly felt apprehensive. Was it safe for her to be with him? After a few moments she waved off her shakiness, knowing that she could not run away at this point even if she was jittery. What did worry her, however, was the possibility of her being sucked into a story too grim to be retold. She gave herself a few seconds to reflect and after a while her nerves calmed down when it occurred to her that what he was saying sounded over the edge. Was he telling the truth or was he fabricating a tale? What parts of his story were real, which a put-on?

"You wanna hear more?"

"I do but before you go on, Rafael, how can I know that what you're telling me really happened?"

"I'm stuck in this loony bin, ain't I?"

"That doesn't mean you're telling me the truth."

"It don't? They say that nuts always tell the truth."

"I haven't heard that before. Anyway, lying comes easy."

"So, you callin' me a liar?"

"No. I only want to be assured that what you're tellin' me isn't made up."

"What do you want? A signed nuthouse certificate tellin' that my story is true?"

"No."

"Well?"

"Go on. Go on. I'm listening."

"Okay. I'll tell you that I still think real hard about what happened to me in the cemetery, when them voices took on a mug and feet and traps. A lotta time has passed since then, but the ugly feeling still sticks to me. I know how close I came to goin' nuts that day.

"Maybe I did go off my rocker. Look around real hard. As I said, I'm in a loony bin. That means that somebody thinks I'm crazy, which means that maybe I did lose it. Just look at the poor sonsabitches and watch how they obey the flunkies that run this place. But I'm the same as everybody else. When I hear *jump*, I jump. When them stooges say, swallow the goddamn pills, that's what I do. What the hell! I do what everybody else does. I grumble and bellyache but I'm obedient, just like a mutt. I'm just another one of the walking stiffs that hang around here like zombies.

"But sometimes I'm different. I keep thinkin' and rememberin' all the time. For instance, I think of Sister Gladys who tol' me that I could call her anytime 'cause she was my friend. Let me tell you that after I got all screwed up in the cemetery, I thought of her for days. I went back to work all right, but my brain was all fucked up while I chewed on the idea of callin' the nun. It wasn't no piece of cake. My head was packed with reasons why I should call her fightin' against why I shouldn't.

"I needed somebody real bad and I knew that I couldn't play it alone no more, not if I wanted to stay alive. But I thought about it in another way, too. I knew that if I went to her I hadda open up, tell her all the shitty things I done since I was a kid. I thought real careful about it and knew that I hadda fess up to her about the weird dreams, the voices, my crazy days with the L.A. bums, my ol' man, and even how much I wanted to snuff out the scumbag. I knew that if I spilled all that crap, she might think I was a freak. I was scared to see her.

"You wanna know when I do most of my rememberin'? It happens when I hear the clang of the big switch at night. Lights out! Click! Just like that! The long room gets real dark 'cept for a little bit of light that creeps in through the monster windows. I see weird lines smeared on the floor, and even the cots lined up look like a buncha dead lizards. That's when

I put my head on the pillow and try to figure out how in the hell I got to this goddamn place. I think so much that I'm still awake when all the other nuts are snorin'. I'm that way till the pills knock me out.

"Nobody knows what it's like to be pumped up with all the shit they give a guy around here. A pill for this, a pill for that! It all goes down my throat and then my brain starts to dance around, all oozy and fucked up. I see shadows and things that slither around my bed and I get spooked! All this happens when it's dark but I hang on to the horses as long as I can just so I can remember.

"That's when it all comes back to me and I remember that before I went to Sister Gladys I made a King Kong mistake. I can't explain why it happened but I got filled up with the idea that I hadda face my ol' man. I wanted to do that even before I saw Gladys. So I went to see him. Yeah! I put my face right into the sonofabitch's mug, can you believe it?

"A few days after I freaked out at the cemetery, I went back to work packin' livers and sausages, all the time tryin' to act like nothin' happened to me. I could tell the guys was gawkin' at me just like they knew somethin' big slammed down on me while I was away. They wanted to stick their long noses into my business, I knew that much, but there wasn't no way they would know. I just kept my life under wraps. Nobody knew what I did on my days off.

"I let them pricks think what they wanted. They coulda thought that I was out on the streets messin' around or that I got wasted or stoned. I didn't give a shit what they thought as long as my life was a secret. But on that day, when I came back from the cemetery, I started gettin' a weird feeling, like I was made of glass and them dickheads could see right through me.

"I still can't explain why I hadda stay all clammed up, 'cept that's the way I was ever since I was a brat. I was real chicken about anybody gettin' a look at my insides and maybe that's why the voices always had such a party with my head. They had me all to themselves. Scumbags! Nobody was there to stand by me while they pulled their shitty games on me. Anyway, it was in the middle of all that crap that I made up my mind to find the ol' man."

"Rafael, had you already talked to Sister Gladys by that time?"

"Yeah! On the phone. She tol' me to come to her place."

"And?"

"I went, but first I made it to the ol' man's place."

"Did you tell Sister Gladys what you were going to do?

"Yeah."

"What did she say about it?"

"She tol' me not to do it."

"But you did it anyway?"

"Yeah. She knew that all I wanted to do was to mix it up with the ol' man so she tol' me to forget it. But I was hot. I couldn't stop myself."

"Weren't you afraid of your feelings?"

"What's that mean?"

"You told me about the time you got filled up with the impulse to kill your father and that the feeling was so strong you got sick over it."

"Oh, yeah! I forgot I tol' you about that time. Well, I just thought it wasn't no big deal. I don't know. Maybe I thought I could hang on to the goddamn horses. What's the difference? It's done. I did it. Wanna hear about it?"

"Yes."

"It was a piece of cake finding him. He lives in Beverly Hills now. You know, that's where the big deals come off the wall just about every day. Can you believe it? Oh, yeah! Maids, swimmin' pool, snotty clubs, fancy wheels, expensive duds, all the crap anybody could think about. That's the ol' man! Money, that's all that matters to him.

"I got the telephone number and punched it out. That's how easy it was and when he came to the phone he acted like nothin' new was happenin', like he forgot the last time we tangled. Without sayin' nothin' about it, he said for me to come see him. His oily voice made me wanna puke but since I started the whole goddamn thing, there wasn't no way I was gonna back down.

"I picked up the bus after work and made it to the ol' man's castle. I don't mind fessin' up that my hand shook when I rang the doorbell and I felt even more spooked when a maid came and opened up. She was a little round Mexican tryin' to sound like she wasn't a wetback and I knew that the ol' man was still up to his ol' tricks. She looked at me and said that my father was waitin' for me.

Mr. Cota is in the kitchen. I'll show you the way.

No thanks. I'll find him myself.

"Ain't that a crock? Who in the hell does he think he is? A movie star or somethin'? Anyway, I followed the smells that came to me outta the kitchen 'cause I knew that's where I'd find him. I shuffled along, not too sure of myself, and I started to feel like a kid again, just rememberin' the days when I lived with him. The place even smelled the same and I almost 'spected to hear the hee-haw of the female hyenas he likes to lay.

"I scraped my feet on the shiny floor. I wanted him to know that I was comin', but when I got to the kitchen he never bothered to look at me. He was mixin' up somethin' in a pot, pretendin' he didn't hear me, but he heard me all right. He hears like a goddamn jackal.

"I stood there watchin' him like I was a moron, not givin' a damn what little game he was playin'. I coulda waited all night if that's what he wanted. I looked at the big whiskey glass on the table and I knew that he was half tanked already. Finally the voice sounded out.

Hello, Rafael.

Hey!

Want a drink?

No.

Don't you want something?

No.

Well, what've you been doing with yourself for the past couple of years?

Five.

Okay. What've you been doing?

This and that.

This and that! Well, I see that some things don't change.

What's that mean?

I hoped you'd say that you've finished school, that you have a diploma or a degree. I'd like to hear that you've returned so we can work together. But I'm not hearing that. I'm hearing nothing. So again I ask you, why did you come? What's the point?

I came to talk to you.

About what?

Rudy. The girls. Rosario.

"Man! Did his eyeballs nearly bug outta that round face of his. He acted just like I kicked him in the balls and when I saw that I smelled blood. I knew I was hot and that I scored big. I thought that nothin' was gonna stop me now!

Don't mention the children. That goes for your mother!

Why the big change? That's all you blabbed about when I was a kid.

Things are different now.

I just wanna talk to you, that's all. What's wrong with that?

You can talk all you want, just remember to keep your boundaries.

Boundaries?

Look, I've had a tough day. I've been looking forward to a quiet drink and a peaceful meal. So if you have nothing else but to stand there babbling like a fool, then let's just call it a day. Okay?

I'll get outta here as soon as you tell me what happened that night. Is that too much to ask? Goddamn it! I'm your son! The only one left alive! I wanna know what happened.

Hey! Watch the bad language and lower your voice! I don't like shouting! Let's just calm down.

Tell me about that night!

"The ol' man's mug started to change. Maybe somethin' he was seein' in me spooked him, or maybe the booze was hittin' him. All I know is that he acted mousy and started to put out.

I can't tell you anything different from what's written in the record. I left the house and your mother killed the kids. She was drunk. When I returned there was nothing I could do but call the police. What else can I tell you?

You're the one who's supposed to know, not me.

Look, you should let go of it. Listen to me, Rafael. Don't you think that I've been haunted by that night as much as you have? Remember, I'm the one who lost the most. I'm the one who has suffered more than anyone else.

"I started to see red spots when he said that. Where did he get the guts to feel sorry for himself like that? Him and his fancy white shorts, his uptight restaurants, the big rings on his ugly fingers! I couldn't hold it in no more and lost it right there.

Fuck you and your bleedin' heart! The kids was the big losers. They was snuffed out! They lost their goddamn life! And what about Rosario? She's been holed up for more than twenty years while you been out free to have your drinks, to dress in your stinking suits, to mess around with your sluts!

"I don't know why, but I got real close to him. He jumped back against the stove and spilled his crappy drink. Damn! Just then, I caught on what a peewee he is. If you think I'm skinny, he's even more sucked up and I knew I could take him easy. I eyeballed him so close that I could see that he was scared shitless and that was like smelling blood for me. I swear! When I first walked into his house, all I wanted was to talk to him but it was too late now. I went blind and all I could hear was the stinkin' voices going off inside my head, screamin' for me to waste him, to carve out his heart. I jumped all over him and mauled the shit outta the scumbag.

"After that, all I remember is the racket of forks and spoons fallin' all over the place. The empty glass flew by his head and exploded against the floor like a bomb. He didn't try to fight back but that only made me madder than hell. We fell. Me on top with my hands squeezin' his skinny neck and the slimy skin felt just like the dead carcasses I shoved around at work. All the time he gurgled like a stuck pig and I wailed like a wild animal. I was a little brat again, scared and pissed and miserable.

"I smashed down my fingers real hard for a long time before I felt hands yankin' at my hair, but I couldn't stop. I kept on squeezin' and squeezin'. Then I felt a goddamn pain in my head and everythin' went black. When I woke up, there was two mugs gawkin' down at me, but they was blurs so I couldn't make out who they was. I rubbed my eyeballs but what I felt most was that my head was gonna explode from the pain. Then I saw that the faces was cops. One of them yanked me to my feet, twisted my arms behind my back, and slapped cuffs on me.

You have the right to remain silent.

"The dude kept on blabbin' but I just stood there feelin' wobbly, just like a stupid idiot. Everythin', even the guy's words, was a big blur. I didn't know where I was till I remembered that I was still in the ol' man's kitchen. When I turned I saw him sittin' on a chair rubbin' his fuckin' neck. After that the coppers hauled me away.

Buddy, this is your lucky day. The maid saved you from murdering the ol' man when she conked you on the noodle with a frying pan. You can thank your lucky stars. As it stands, it's only assault and battery. It coulda been homicide.

"Ain't that too much? Busted for tryin' to waste the ol' man, but I missed! I couldn't even pull it off right! What the hell! I didn't fight back. I was too beat up, so I let the cop shove me into the back of the cruiser and I rolled up on the seat, tryin' to forget the pain in my head.

"Then the cop at the wheel peeled away from the curb like the mob was hot on his ass but I looked out the back window anyway, just in time to see the ol' man climbin' into another black and white. It was a fast look but I seen that he was on his feet. I didn't even put a nick into that ol' carcass."

CHAPTER 15

Next day Elena Santos sat waiting for Rafael; traffic had been light that morning and she was early. She welcomed the quiet time because she was having a hard time shaking off the turmoil that had come over her after hearing Rafael's description of the assault on his father. It was not that she had not known about it. In fact, she had read several accounts of the episode. However, it was the tone of his voice, his choice of words, and even his gestures that had churned her up.

She told herself that she should have left it alone, but she did not. When she returned to her apartment, she replayed the tape not once but several times, and listening to his words robbed her of sleep again. She sighed, admitting that she was shaken.

"Hi!"

"Hello, Rafael."

"Back for more?"

Elena caught Rafael's mocking tone. Resenting his rudeness, she bluntly answered his cutting remark, not caring how he would react.

"Sure. Let's get right to it, but first I'd like you to say some words about why you hate your father so much."

"What's that mean?"

"Just that it's necessary to explain why a son tries to murder his father without reason."

"You gotta be kiddin'. He's a sonofabitch!"

"That's not necessarily apparent to others. He took care of you, tried to educate you, gave you shelter only to have you walk out on him. It's difficult to see right off why you tried to kill him except out of nastiness on your part."

"I ain't gonna sit here and take this crap!"

"Suit yourself."

Rafael rolled back into the chair, hunched over, morose and pouting, but instead of walking out he bit his nails. He would not look at Elena who kept her eyes on him, expecting him to leave and possibly not return. She knew she had put her finger on a raw nerve but she did not regret it. After a while she leaned close to him and spoke. Her voice was low, nearly a whisper.

"Rafael, will you tell me why you hate him so much?"

"I don't know, I just do."

"Do you feel bad about trying to kill him?"

"No."

"It never bothers you to think about it?"

"No."

"You've made me think that he murdered the children. Do you really believe that?"

"Yeah."

"Why?"

"I don't know, I just do."

"Could it be that you don't want to accept that it was your mother who did it?"

"Goddamn it! It wasn't Rosario!"

He was now shouting, forcing Elena to realize that pursuing this path might truly lose him once and for all so she retreated, deciding to take a safer route. There was still much to hear of Rafael's story, details of how he got to see his mother and what finally brought him to this place. This led her to think that the best thing for her would be to leave the darker part of his life to his doctors.

"Okay. Let's talk about her. What was taking so long to get the clearance to see her?"

"I got the green light."

"When?"

"I don't remember exactly when, but it came."

"Before you beat up your father?"

"Yeah."

"Before you met Sister Gladys the first time?"

"Somewhere around that time."

"Why didn't you mention it to me?"

"I did."

"No. You didn't."

"Okay. So I forgot. What of it?"

"Well, I would have asked you why you didn't go straight to see her before anything else."

"And I woulda tol' you that I wanted to know more before I saw her. I wanted to check out more scoop from Sister Gladys."

"Rafael, I thought you said that you contacted the sister because you didn't want to be alone, not to get more information out of her."

"Well, that's about it."

Elena leaned back in the chair and closed her eyes, knowing that Rafael was leading her in circles. She realized that whatever specific information he was giving her was coming in disconnected pieces and, what was more important, that those fragments would not come out of him unless she asked the right questions, at the right moment. She straightened up, deciding to pursue the tangled road she was on regardless of the difficulties.

"Have you seen your father since that day?"

"Yeah. Right there in the jailhouse."

"You mean you were jailed together?"

"Nope. I saw him on the outside."

"When you were released?"

"Yeah."

"That same day?"

"Yeah. The ol' man dropped the charges. I found when the guards shoved me from the holding cell into the big waiting room. God! I was sore all over and my ass was freezin'. It's no fun spendin' a night trapped with all them winos and freaks, but when the dickhead in charge tol' me to hit the road, I didn't take a minute to ask why. All I knew was that I could get the hell outta there and that's what I did.

"I was all wobbly and dazed when I made it to the big waiting room filled with a buncha losers stickin' around to get their shit fixed. The coppers gave me one phone call, so I contacted Sister Gladys and she tol' me to sit tight till she got there. That's what I did, even if I was starvin' and freezin'.

"I found a spot between a fat bitch and a one-legged bugger who was sittin' on the bench pinchin' a scab on his arm. I didn't give a damn. The place was so filled up that I jumped at the empty place without thinkin' nothin' 'cept that I wanted Sister Gladys to come for me right away. The spot was close to the door, so I figured I could see her the minute she came. In the meantime the hurt in my head was so bad that I hadda close my eyes, tryin' to forget it. Once or twice I touched where the no-good maid landed the pan on my head and my fingers felt a ball on my head stickin' straight up in the air. It hurt like hell!

"A long time passed but Sister Gladys didn't show. My belly was kickin' up a fuss and everythin' was hurtin' me real bad, but I was tryin' to hang in there, just waitin' with my peepers shut tight. Then one time when I opened them I saw him. I caught the ol' man slitherin' outta one of the little rooms, headin' straight for the door.

"It was him for sure and he was runnin' like a jackrabbit with its ass on fire. He pushed on the glass door and disappeared. Just like that! First he was there and then he wasn't. At first I couldn't be sure it was him so I ran after him. I hadda take a real hard look 'cause I thought I saw somethin' that I couldn't believe. It looked like his hair had turned all white and I hadda make sure. Maybe the fat egg on my head was playin' tricks on my eyeballs.

"I got to the door just in time to see him jump into a cop cruiser, but it was enough for me to see that I was right. The hair on that big head of his had turned white! It wasn't the wad on my skull that was tellin' me that and it wasn't even the ugly lights in the room. I saw it right there in the sun, the mop on his head had turned all white. Can you believe that? It happened overnight, right there in the goddamn jailhouse.

"The seat next to the one-legged freak was still empty, so I went back to sit and think, tryin' to remember what the ol' man looked like the night before. Maybe I was wrong. Maybe his hair was already white, but the more I thought about it the more I knew that it was more black, with just a little bit of white. Now I saw that he turned into a real ol' bum, just like the winos on skid row. I mean he was all bony and shriveled up, making me think his fancy shorts would fall off his ass. I started to laugh just thinkin' what all them big-tit bitches of his would do when they saw him. For sure, they was gonna hit the road in the other direction. Served him right!

"Then a spooky thought hit me. What if I got all shriveled up that night in the jailhouse just like the ol' man? What if my hair was white and my face wrinkled like a prune? I got so goddamn scared that I almost asked the one-legged bugger what I looked like, but instead I ran to the toilet just to look at myself in a mirror. I stood there gawkin' at myself like a stinkin' retard, but I saw that I was the same ugly son-of-a-bitch. Nothing had changed.

"I went back to wait for Sister Gladys, but I was startin' to feel real funny. Somethin' weird was taking over me. I was feelin' like chickenshit thinkin' the ol' man was just a broken-down piece of crap and still I mauled him like I did the bitch, the one I wasted for rippin' off my cardboard box."

Elena glared at Rafael. He reacted by shifting in the chair, rubbing his hands, and nervously kicking his foot in midair. Neither spoke but their silence was heavy, leading Elena to expect an outburst from him. When he kept quiet, she took the lead.

"You were feeling ashamed."

"What?"

"You heard me."

"Why should I be ashamed? He had it comin', didn't he?"

"But you were stronger."

"That ain't got nothin' to do with it!"

"You're his son."

"What's that gotta do with it?"

"A son is supposed to respect his father."

"Where'd you pick up that kinda bullshit?"

"If it didn't mean anything, why were you feeling bad about it?"

"I said that I started to feel funny, not bad. That feeling stopped when I remembered that he ain't nothin' but a piece of crap."

"Yet a while ago you called the whole thing a big mistake, didn't you?"

"Yeah."

"Well?"

"I call it a big mistake 'cause I didn't finish the job. I let the ol' bastard go. That's the big boo-boo."

Rafael leaned back, hands cuffed over his mouth, and his shoulders shook with laughter while he glared at Elena with slanted, flinty eyes filled with mockery. He gave her the impression that he was laughing at her, that the joke was on her and that he was enjoying every second of her confusion. She felt a wave of exasperation come over her because now she did not know what to believe. He was jeering and having a lot of fun; that was the only clear thing.

"So the part about his hair turning white is a big joke, isn't it?"

"Nope! It happened."

"I don't believe you! You're putting me on."

"I tell you it's the goddamn real truth! His hair turned white. How come I'd put you on?"

"Just like you've put me on about the big mistake."

"Can't you take a joke?"

"You see? It is a joke and you're laughing at me."

"No, it's the truth! I just feel like takin' a little laugh. Why are you so fucked up over it?"

Elena had had enough and reached for her things intending to leave. She was fatigued and fed up with Rafael. She needed to get away from him, go home, have a drink, put on the television, and just hear the latest gossip on the local news. She did not want to be with him anymore.

"Look! I know you're feelin' salty, but just relax. Let me tell you about Sister Gladys, I'm almost there. I can tell you that part real easy. Remember I was waitin' for her when the ol' man sidetracked me? Wanna hear?"

"Go ahead, Rafael, but remember I'm tired and I'm not going to sit around listening to more fooling around."

"I was sittin' by the one-legger when somebody called out my name. I stretched my neck every which way but I couldn't see who the hell was callin' me. Then I heard it again and there she was, standin' in front of me lookin' like Mighty Mouse with a buncha papers hangin' from her hands. I jumped up like a jackrabbit. I was waitin' for her but I couldn't figure out how the hell she coulda been standin' in front of me and I didn't see her. You know what I mean? I started blabbin' my head off.

Sister! Jesus, thanks for comin'.

I could not have done otherwise and don't take the name of the Lord in vain. Come on! You've been cleared. We'll talk in the car.

"She grabbed my arm and we shot outta there like bats sprung from hell, but when I hit the light, my eyeballs started blinkin' and sneezes choked me up somethin' awful. I wanted to stop but she didn't care. She kept walkin' so fast I

thought her legs was pistons. She never stopped for nothin'
'cept to say hi to all her copper buddies.

Hi there, Sister! Where ya been all this time?

Keeping busy, Harry. Just keeping out of trouble.

Way to go!

Hey, Sister! We miss you! Long time no see!

Old rocking chair's got me, Ollie.

Ha! That'll be the day.

Who's your buddy?

An old friend!

"Aint that a crock? Me? A friend? I knew I was in for a trip
with her, but I hung in there. I caught on that she knew her
way around the place, like she visited the jailbirds all the time.
She pointed that way and that's where I went. She pulled the
other direction and there I was, right behind her till we got
to her jalopy. I stood lookin' at it while she opened the doors.
It was so faded that I couldn't tell what color it was and the
rear end of the thing was all bent in. I thought that I wouldn't
drive that heap of junk even to the worst part of my ol' barrio. I guess she got into what was goin' on in my brain 'cause
soon as I sat down she looked at me and let loose a big ol'
smile. She looked like a cat.

*It's old and battered, Rafael, but it gets me around. This
little Datsun has made a round trip cross-country and gone up
and down California many times. Don't look down on it just
because it's small and faded. It still has a lot of miles in it.*

"We pulled outta the parking lot, burnin' rubber all the
way south on the freeway, and then headed east straight for
her convent. The built-in egg on my head was a bummer,
hurtin' me big-time, so I put my head where there wasn't a
crack in the backrest and pretended to be sleepin'. It was
kinda hard. That sister was drivin' like crazy, but I hung in
there, thinkin' of how I almost wasted the ol' man the night
before. Yeah! You're givin' me the eagle eye and I know what

you're thinkin', but what can I say? It's for real. I was thinkin' about it and I hadda talk.

Sister?

Yes?

I tried to kill my ol' man.

I know. The supervisor in charge of the night shift told me about it.

It's serious, ain't it?

It could have been.

How come the cops didn't pinch me?'

Because your father dropped the charges.

Yeah, I know. Why'd he do that?

That's for you to think about, Rafael. Maybe you won't be able to do it right away, but in time you must find the meaning of your father's actions.

"I made out like I was goin' back to sleep, but the more I thought of it, the more messed up I got. I just couldn't get it. The ol' man coulda put me away behind bars for a long time. It just didn't fit in with his no good ways but I couldn't find the angle no matter how hard I looked. I tol' myself that maybe I just scared the shit outta him so bad that he went off his rocker. Maybe. Still, there was no way I coulda trusted the son-of-a-bitch. Somethin' was wrong but I couldn't figure it out, so when I got tired of tryin' I gave up. I shut my eyes and thought of the ache in my head till Sister Gladys started talkin' again.

Wake up, Rafael, we're here. I'll take you to our guest room where you can shower and sleep. In the meantime, I'll find some fresh clothes for you in the used clothes bin. The stuff we have there is all hand-me-down, but it's clean and in better shape than what you've got on.

"We got outta the heap and I walked behind her like a lost alley cat while she took me to a little room. Even if my eyeballs was all blurry, I could see it was a nice place to crash. It had a bed and even a toilet and shower.

Take a long shower, Rafael. Try to sleep. When you wake up you'll find something to put on. I'll leave it right here on this chair. After that, we'll have dinner and talk.

"Do this! Do that! She was like a little cop, pushin' me around, givin' me orders. But I didn't care. I was too beat up. She stomped over to the window and pulled down the shades till the room was dark, then she patted my arm and walked away. I took off my clothes and got under the shower for a long time while I thought of the kick-ass pain in my head.

"There was more that I was thinkin' beside the egg on my head. I couldn't get rid of the stinkin' feeling of the ol' man's neck under my fingers. I kept rememberin' the flabby skin slippin' around just like a chicken neck. What pissed me most was that the ol' bugger didn't fight back. How come?

"I stayed under the water for a long time just in case the feeling would wash off me, but it wouldn't go away. Then I shook my body and arms from my head down to my feet, just like the fleabag mutts did when I dumped water on 'em, but there was no way I could shake off the feeling, so I gave up again.

"I got outta the shower and went straight to the bed where I fell into a weird sleep. I say weird 'cause it was empty. This time I didn't see the stinkin' murders all over again. It was all quiet in the dream. Nobody was yellin' or cryin'. I didn't even dream of the big hit on my head, or the ol' man's goddamn chicken skin under my fingers. I just fell into a deep, black hole with nothin' in it.

"When I woke up I kinda thought that Sister Gladys would be there, but she wasn't. I didn't know what time it was but I saw that there was just a little bit of light under the shades. I knew it was gonna be night real soon but I didn't jump outta the bed. I just kicked back and thought of how weird it was that I didn't dream about nothin'.

"Then it hit me that for just that one time my brain was quiet, that it didn't have no voices kickin' my ass all over the place. I couldn't even hear myself yellin' when I jumped the ol' man. It was real quiet in there and I kinda liked it. I started thinkin' that maybe Sister Gladys was right in the first place when she tol' me not to go see the ol' man. I almost whacked the bastard! What if that happened? I would be in the can for sure by now. I almost did it, and I woulda done it 'cept the maid clipped me good, but the real thing was that I wanted to kill him. So if wantin' to snuff out somebody was a crime, then I belonged in the slammer just like Rosario.

"Thinkin' of bein' cooped up made me remember the night I spent in the can. I even felt how the goddamn guards shoved me into the tank, a monster place crammed to the edges with broken-down degenerates. The smell was godawful, nearly makin' me puke while I squeezed in between bodies till I finally found a corner by myself. That's where I squatted the whole stinkin' night, coverin' my head with my arms so I didn't have to catch all them ugly eyes lookin' at me like I was a real slimebag.

"I tried to sleep but the racket in the cage clanged away at the big ball on my head, makin' it feel like hammers was bangin' away at me. A couple of times I looked around and saw nothin' but a buncha scumbags, all worse off than me, howlin', mumblin', bellyachin', and even cryin' like snivelin' brats. I shook all over. At first I thought I was cold but then I knew that I was spooked outta my gourd, just like the rest of them pricks. The hours dragged till some dickhead in uniform yanked me outta that hole and tol' me that I got one phone call. That's when I called Sister Gladys.

"It was dark by the time my brain came back to the little room in the convent, so I jumped outta the bed and saw a pile of clothes, even shorts, on the chair. When I was all set I walked out to wait for Sister Gladys in the spooky hall."

Elena sat back thinking of Rafael's words but when the recorder clicked off she interrupted her thoughts, taking it as her moment to leave. She was more tired than ever and it had grown dark outdoors. If she was to beat the heavy traffic, she had better leave.

"Rafael, when we meet tomorrow I want you to skip ahead to when you visited your mother."

"Don't you wanna hear more about Sister Gladys?"

"I find her interesting, but covering her story will take more time than I had planned."

"Why are you always in such a big hurry?"

"I'm not in a big hurry, but I do want to get to what I believe my readers want to know and that's the encounters with your mother."

"Your readers? I thought it was my story, not yours."

"It *is* your story, but I'm the one who's writing it."

"Does that make you the boss?"

"Rafael, stop playing this game. I'm tired and you know it, that's why you're acting like a brat."

"I ain't actin' like a brat! It's you that's actin' like a bitch!"

Elena got to her feet, not in haste or even with a show of irritation because she knew that was what Rafael expected. Instead, she gathered her things calmly.

"Good-night, Rafael. We'll continue tomorrow and if what you've got to say about Sister Gladys adds to your story, well then, that's where we'll pick up."

CHAPTER 16

"Hi! I'm glad you came and that you're not bent outta shape. I'm sorry I called you a bitch yesterday. I didn't mean it. I'm a real asshole and my trap runs off. So what if we just get down to the story even if you don't wanna hear this part about Sister Gladys. She stood by me when I was gettin' up the nerve to see Rosario and that night with Sister has lots to do with it. That's why you should hear it.

"It was late in the night, when we was the only ones awake, the only ones still talkin'. We was in the middle of a room that was all dark except for a lamp that spread a big circle around us. It was there that we talked for a long time.

"I opened up to someone for the first time ever. I guess I woulda done it with Abuela but she was gone by then. Words came outta my mouth like a river and once I started nothin' coulda stopped me, I just let it all hang out. I talked so goddamn much that I even spooked myself.

"I fessed up about the cockeyed years when I was a snotty kid and all the scary dreams I got almost all the time. I even tol' her how I pissed my bed just about every night. I talked about the only thing I loved in my life: Abuela, her garden, and stories. I spilled everythin' about my ol' man and how I hated his guts. I let out how I screwed around the L.A. streets stoned outta my gourd, stealin' and pushin' around any asshole that couldn't push back. I tol' her my secret: that I was gonna prove Rosario is innocent and that I even had the paper that tol' me that I could visit her. After a while I shut up, but then I started all over again.

"I kept the worse for the last. I didn't want the sister to know but it squeezed out anyway. I tol' her about the goddamn voices and how they almost did me in when I was in the

148

cemetery. My trap ran off like a motor, but all the time Sister Gladys never stopped me. Her little peepers blinked a lot and she moved her butt on the chair, crossin' and uncrossin' her skinny bird legs.

"When I finally shut up she stayed real quiet, she didn't move no more. I kinda closed my eyes to make her think that I was fallin' asleep but I was checkin' her out. Just when I thought she was gonna fall asleep herself, I heard her take a big gulp of air, like she was goin' underwater or somethin'.

Rafael, thank you for telling me all of this. It means a lot because I sense that you hardly ever speak with anyone about yourself. You've done the right thing. I'm your friend.

Sister, sometimes I think I'm goin' outta my gourd, 'specially now that I tried to zap the ol' man. I can't shake a weird feeling off my fingers. I feel his goddamn neck wobblin'.

Rafael, may I ask a favor of you?

Yeah.

Please watch your language. I'm sure you can speak without taking God's name in vain or even using other ugly words. Will you do me that favor?

Yeah! Sorry! I'll try.

Thank you! Now, what you were saying about the feeling on your hands, I can say that it's understandable. You've attempted to kill your father and yet he's forgiven you.

You mean he dropped the charges.

That's forgiveness.

I don't think it was forgiveness. It was just easier.

Easier? I'm going to tell you something few people know about my own father and how he forgave me. My family is from Texas. We've been natives of that state for about four or five generations on my mother's side. It turned out different on my father's side. He was a native of Mexico where he was born in a little northern town by the name of Nuevo Progreso.

When he was about fifteen or sixteen years old he was swept up by the revolution that was going full blast by that time. He was good at playing the bugle so he joined the hordes of fighting men, following them up and down Mexico, sounding battle signals. He did this until he got fed up with the carnage. One day he picked up his knapsack and walked in the opposite direction until he reached the border. He crossed into Tucson. From there he made his way to Texas where he met my mother.

He joined her family, the Amescua clan, and he became so much a part of them that he never again looked back to Mexico even though it meant forgetting his own family. He became a rancher when he was able to get a small piece of land and there he and my mother began their life together while they had us. I'm the youngest of seven kids.

I'm telling you his story so you know that he was a good man and that I wasn't a good daughter. To this day I still can't explain why I resented him so much. I think I even hated him most of the time. I say I can't explain it because, as I said, he was a good man. He treated his children well, he provided, he was a loving husband, but still I had a bad feeling for him here in my heart.

In time, this dislike became so intense that I could hardly be in the same room with him and my bad feelings showed because everyone could tell how I felt about him. My mother would scold me one day and then sweet-talk me later, but nothing changed my heart. I couldn't stand him and as I grew I saw how deeply it hurt him. When I discovered the effect on him of what I did, instead of changing I did it even more. As you can guess, in time my behavior got to him and finally alienated him from me until he, too, showed resentment toward me.

I was about eighteen when I decided to become a nun. Isn't that ironic? How was I to dedicate myself to a life in which love of others is the highest calling if my heart was loaded with aversion for my father? Yet I did it. Maybe my real motive was to get away from him because in those days a girl didn't have too many options, so I chose the convent.

When I left home I didn't even bother to say good-bye to him, but by that time he didn't let my rudeness hurt him. I heard later that he said he was glad that I had left the family. For my part, I took the train that brought me all the way to the coast of California to Gonzales and I never looked back. Ultimately I became a nun and a grammar school teacher. How did I feel inside all along? Not good, Rafael, because I knew that I had offended him unjustly. I tried to forget and the years passed as they always do, helping my feelings to calm down.

During the fifties an epidemic hit most of the country. It was the flu, not the big influenza that hit after the first war, but still, it was a very serious version. I caught it and nearly died, as did some people. In fact, the doctor that attended those of us who had fallen ill said that I had only a few days to live.

I didn't take that sickness bravely. I was a coward. I didn't want to die and cried and wailed. In the meantime our Mother Superior notified my father. My mother had died by that time. Although already very old and frail, he traveled on a bus all those miles just to come to my side. He arrived in time to find me still alive and he sat by my bed day and night, taking the risk of catching the illness.

A miracle must have happened because my fever broke and I pulled out. When I regained consciousness, I found him sitting there, drained and looking sick. I remember feeling so ashamed and humiliated looking at that old man, frail and crumpled, keeping his daughter company as she fought for her life. He never left my side; he stayed there night and day. It was then that my heart changed. That, more than regaining health, was the real miracle. My heart had actually been transformed from the hardness of stone to the softness of flesh.

A while ago you spoke of not being able to rid yourself of your father's struggling throat under your fingers. Well, I'll tell you that I've never been able to erase the image of that old man sitting in a chair by my side. I see him often.

When he saw that I had come back, he reached out his hand and put it on mine and I saw in his eyes that he had forgiven me. His presence told me so, more than words. I understood. Another thing that penetrated me at that moment was that forgiving me could not have been easy for him, that it must have cost him a lot. It wasn't easy.

Rafael, you and I share a resentment of our fathers. Oh, I know it's for different reasons and in different ways and measures. Nonetheless, if we don't erase it, that bitterness will inhibit our heart; it will shrink it.

What're you saying, Sister?

I'm saying that rancor is a deadly thing, no matter where it comes from. I'm saying that it deadens our insides if we don't get rid of it.

Rancor? What's that?

It means holding a deep grudge.

You think I can kick it? I can never stop feelin' pissed at that ol' man.

Maybe. But I also think that by dropping the charges, your father is trying to tell you something.

What?

That he's sorry.

That's a lotta bull!

I think that only by accepting his regret will you be able to forgive him.

Forgive him! Why should I forgive him? He messed up my mother's life. Mine, too.

I already said it. Forgiving is very hard, maybe the hardest thing to do in life. But keep in mind that you tried to kill him, which is very serious, and he forgave you. I know that what he's done has hurt you deeply, but forgiveness has to begin with someone. Let it be with you.

"Ain't that a crock? The sister really wanted me to forgive that asshole after all he pulled on Rosario and me! The only reason I didn't come out and tell her, in the words that were burnin' my insides, was because I knew that she was tryin' to help me. But honest to God, she was so wrong I almost started yellin' in her face. Instead, I shut my trap and waited for her to go on with her story, but then she made a U-turn and hit me up in another direction.

One of my sisters and colleagues, Sister Ruth Marie, is an expert in counseling and psychiatry. Her lectures and books enjoy a fine reputation nationally and internationally. She's often invited from as far away as Europe and Africa to conduct seminars. Sister Ruth Marie works with individuals and groups. I know that if I speak to her she'll meet with you.

What do you mean, Sister?

My meaning is that I believe that someone like Sister Ruth Marie can be helpful to you.

Don't you wanna talk to me no more?

I don't mean that at all. What I want you to understand is that I don't have the training or the experience to guide you beyond what I've already said.

Why are you going chicken on me, Sister?

I'm not going chicken on you!

You gave up on Rosario and now you're givin' up on me.

Oh, you're being unfair to me. How do you know that I've given up on your mother? I apologize for giving you the wrong impression, but the truth is that I do want to continue speaking with you and helping you. That's my intention.

Me, too. I'm sorry for gettin' all outta shape. I'm pretty jumpy about things. I didn't mean to come down on your case. I just need to find out the truth.

The truth! There are many truths and many roads leading to those different truths. It's possible to turn the wrong corner while on one of those roads. It's easy to get lost and come across a truth we least want to discover.

What if Rosario is guilty? That's it, ain't it?

Yes.

That ain't gonna happen.

Rafael, it's the past. Let it rest. Aren't you afraid of destroying whatever chance there is for you to have a healthy life? Consider ending the road you're on and embarking on a new one.

You lost me.

A while ago you revealed your experience in the cemetery, where you had fancied your brother and sisters leading a new and good life in another world. Well, Rafael, you can find that same good life right here in this world if only you look to your intelligence and determination and use them to form that new life. That's the road I'm talking about.

I can't drop what I been doin'. I gotta keep goin'.

That road could be dangerous and frightening. Its end might not be a good one for you.

Lookin' for the killer of the kids is what I'm all about.

Let's stop right here. You've said that you want to prove your mother innocent. Now you're saying you're looking for the killer. How are you going to do that? The case would have to be reopened and new convincing evidence has to be established to do that. To do this, sharp lawyers and money are necessary. Rafael, it hurts me to be blunt, but you have neither.

Watch me! I'll do it!

I understand that this has been your purpose, but a purpose is not made of stone, it lives here in our heart, it's made of flesh and it can change. If that purpose is too dangerous or even harmful to anyone, then a new one should be found.

I can't change what's inside me.

You can't or you won't?

What's the difference?

"When I said this Sister Gladys backed off all of a sudden. She looked like she was beat real bad and didn't have no plans to go on fightin' me. I didn't like the look on her face but there was nothin' I could do about it.

I give in to you, Rafael. You've defeated me. What's your next step?

I'm goin' to Quentin to see Rosario.

What?

You can help me, Sister. Will you?

I don't know. She's on death row. Very few people are allowed in to speak with the condemned.

I tol' you I already have the permit. Will you gimme a hand?

My God! You've ground me down to my last drop of strength. Will you show me the ropes?

Rafael, before I answer let me say in the strongest way that I believe that it's a huge mistake for you to go ahead with such a plan.

Why? She's my mother. Ain't it natural for me to wanna see her?

Yes, it's natural, but you've been clear about what you're expecting and you might not get it. You're looking for her to come out and say, "Your father murdered the children." What if that doesn't happen?

She's gonna fess up. I know that for sure.

Listen to me, Rafael. Your mother has been imprisoned for nearly twenty-five years; all the while her spirit has doubtlessly withered. She has suffered through the anxieties and false hopes that the appeals process brings to all prisoners. She has lived among hardened, lonely women, people who have murdered and maimed other human beings. She has been among those who have given up all hope. She, along with the others, has learned that lying is the only way to survive and now you expect her to tell you the truth? You expect this even though she hasn't seen you since you were a baby? If this is your hope, you're setting yourself up for certain disaster. I'm being blunt, I know, but if you truly want my help you will have to hear this and even harder things.

She'll fess up.

I see that you're unmovable. Fine, but remember that despite the harshness I've just described, your mother still has feelings. I want you to consider what effect seeing you will have on her. She's no longer young. She's easily close to seventy and this, too, must be important to you.

No problem.
What about your own frame of mind? What about the voices? You're not strong.
Hey! I'm okay.
Rafael, you worry me very, very much!
Lighten up, Sister. Everythin's cool.
Rafael, I'm going to ask you to help me do what I do best.
Sure. Anythin'.
Let's pray.
I ain't prayed since Abuela. I don't remember how to do it.
Hold my hand, I'll help you remember.
"Then Gladys took my hands. At first my fingers was like frozen sticks, but real soon they started to warm up. Then we prayed."

CHAPTER 17

Elena listened as Rafael told of Sister Gladys's role in his life, feeling grateful that he had ignored her wish to skip telling that part of his story. Thinking over the nun's words, it hit Elena that had he followed through on the sister's advice his life might be different now. The night of his meeting with Sister Gladys had been a crossroad of choices for him, but Rafael chose the wrong turn when he disregarded her words.

"Sister Gladys said important things to you that night."

"Yeah, I guess."

"Didn't you think her telling you about her father meant anything? It was very personal, after all."

"Maybe. I caught on to what she was tellin' me, but to tell you the truth, I kinda thought she was makin' up all that crap about her ol' man just to change my mind."

"You didn't believe her?"

"Well, it sounded mushy, kinda fake. All that talk about a revolution. What did that have to do with me? Somethin' about her words came across screwy. It just didn't hang together."

"Like what?"

"Like the part when the ol' man traveled the whole god-damn country just to sit by her bed. That was stupid!"

"You don't think a father would do that?"

"Not my ol' man. That slimebag would let me croak before he'd come two inches."

"Not all fathers are alike."

"Maybe. Anyway, I let the sister's sob story fly by me."

"What about what she said about keeping a grudge?"

"Well, what do you 'spect from a female?"

"What does that mean?"

"That bitches think different from guys."

"Look, that's enough of that kind of talk! Let's go on with your story. What came next?"

"Back to the rush job, right? Okay, I'll go along with the little game since I'm almost gettin' to like all this stuff anyway."

"Is that the way you really feel about what you're telling me?"

"Well, if I dig down deep I guess there's somethin' different. Lookin' back, I gotta admit you're right and that Sister Gladys was tryin' to tell me somethin'. But I didn't pay no attention to her. I jumped right down the goddamn sewer thinkin' that I knew what was what. I know now that everythin' that happened to me was my fault. I was clammed up and alone, with all that crap buried deep inside me.

"After that night with the sister, I was feelin' real edgy just gettin' ready to see Rosario, but I kept it to myself. Not that the stinkin' voices returned. No, that ain't it. Them slimebags had slinked away since I got serious about takin' the trip to Quentin. The pricks slipped underground, kept their traps shut, and they didn't come back since that day in the cemetery. I guess I spooked them with the idea of seein' Rosario and that tol' me that the little shitheads didn't want me to get together with her. But I wasn't home free. There was still some major things buggin' me, like I was havin' trouble concentratin' at work. I didn't get no sleep and I hated eatin'.

"It was just about that time that I put together a buncha stuff on Quentin. It was a bundle of pictures and shit like that and it was bringin' up a lotta misery in me. Look, that stuff might as well be right here on my lap but it don't matter that it really ain't here anymore. The pages are burned into my brain.

"It took me time, but once I put this bundle together I carried it with me all the time, starin' at the pages without letup. It didn't make no difference if I was on the bus, at lunch break, and most of all when I was alone. Each time I did this my hands shook and my mouth got dry but still I looked at every goddamn paper inside the file. I was afraid of openin' the thing but I did it. I even lost count of the times I done it. Yeah, this is one of the things that got me real sick and I did it to myself.

"Rafael, what was in the file?"

"Well, it was pictures of the inside of Quentin, where Rosario was holed up. They was fuzzy and faded but anyone could see what they was all about. I stared at the holding cells where the jailbirds waited to be fried. The long bars made it easy to see the ugly toilet bowl and stinkin' bunk bed. That showed me where Rosario lived, at least that's what I tol' myself.

"I got four or five of them pictures and I looked and looked at 'em till I felt my goddamn eyeballs almost blow outta their sockets, but what really nailed me was lookin' at the pictures showin' the green room where the poor slobs are fried. There was even a shot of the place where the vultures watched. Can you believe it? Newspaper and TV slimebags hang around just to gawk at somebody gettin' wasted.

"I read somewhere in them pages that it's up to the loser jailbird to choose how to burn. They got a choice between gettin' it in the arm or smellin' a powerful shit till they croak. A choice? That's a choice? Anyway, the place is set up for the two ways of snuffin' out the bugger and the pictures are there for anybody to see.

"The table where the jailbird gets the needle is flat, with a cushion and the straps that tie down the poor slob are colored blood red. Ain't that a crock? But if the bugger chooses to sniff up the gas, he gets to sit on a chair set up with straps and even a place for his arms and legs.

"I looked at them goddamn pictures so long and so much that I nearly lost my marbles. Sometimes I saw Rosario layin' on the table with her arms and legs tied down, her eyes lookin' up at the metal ceiling of the green place. Sometimes I saw her tied on the chair, this time her legs and arms pinned down like she was a hog ready to be butchered. I saw her lookin' through the window at the vultures waitin' to see her croak.

"I felt so scared for Rosario that most of the time my tongue spiked hard and I couldn't talk. I couldn't help myself. The pull to look at them ugly pictures was just too big. This was what was goin' on inside me when I was gettin' ready to see Rosario. Before going to Quentin, I looked at them goddamn pictures so much that I started to see myself walkin' into Rosario's cell for the first time just to talk to her. I saw the bars on one side and a stinkin' little cot with a bowl where she washed her hands. What blew my mind was the toilet stuck on a wall. I couldn't stand the idea of her takin' a crap in front of everybody.

"Then I saw myself standin' in front of her while she stared real hard at my face and body. I didn't know if she'd put her arms around me or just shake my hand or maybe nothin' would happen. Why should she touch a slob like me? That's what ate at me real bad. After thinkin' this way, I tol' myself that I was all messed up. How did I know what the hell was gonna happen anyway? The real thing would probably be different, but I shook all over just thinkin' about it. I was like a zombie.

"I had a real hard time at night when the pictures came back. Over and over I saw those sonsabitches haulin' Rosario into the green room. I didn't get no sleep and most of the time my eyes was peeled wide open when morning light crept through the window in my room. I just couldn't stop thinkin' of her face, her eyes, and I even tried to get inside her brain to see what the hell she was thinkin'.

"Every goddamn night I waited for midnight. Even if it was all in my head I knew that's when she was gonna be zapped. I kept my eye on the clock by my bed, watchin' the thing tick, tick, tick, just like her life slippin' away little by little. I could see her in the shitty jumpsuit and the big shoes that was gonna be pulled off before she got strapped on the flat bed. I saw the straps cuttin' into her arms and her fingers openin' and shuttin', beggin' me to come help her. I saw her eyes glued on the window where the vultures hung their goddamn beaks, shuttin' and closin' them, waitin' for the kill. I knew all this was happenin' 'cause I was standin' next to 'em and caught the whole fuckin' picture.

"Then the hand of the clock reached midnight and I felt my heart yank at my ribs, tryin' to jump outta its cage. The clock would blow up like a giant wheel, clickin', eatin' its way to snuff out Rosario. The thing never stopped, it just kept movin' and movin'. Each goddamn tick filled me up with so much sadness that I couldn't hardly breathe. It hurt so much that I hated Rosario for doin' this to me. I put the pillow over my big mouth and bawled like a little kid. I cried 'cause I hated her and loved her at the same time."

Rafael's voice dropped off. Elena looked at him, realizing that he was deeply shaken but she did not know what to say. She tried to imagine what he had gone through but it was no use. She knew it was impossible for her to feel what he felt. She decided that even though she was anxious to hear of the meeting with his mother, it would be too much to push on. She asked a last question.

"Do you still have these thoughts, Rafael?"

"Nope. The pills get me through the night."

"Let's call it quits for today. Okay? I'll return at the usual time. What do you think?"

"Yeah. My head is hurting."

"I hope you get enough sleep."

"See you tomorrow."

CHAPTER 18

"Sister Gladys and me hit the road early one morning, and that skinny chicken leg of hers slammed down hard on the pedal. We never stopped 'cept when we hadda take a leak or grab somethin' to eat. We drove up the coast till we got to Quentin just about sunset. She rolled the Datsun into a beat-up motel where we stayed, waitin' for the next morning. I couldn't sleep, afraid of what the hell was gonna happen when I saw Rosario.

"Next day we made it up the hill to the pen, cleared all the gates, but when we got to the main door Sister Gladys split in a different direction. I was alone all over again but that was cool with me. I knew that's how I hadda face Rosario. I took a big gulp of air and did my slow walk up to the counter where a big white dude in a uniform stood eyeballin' me. He was packin' but that didn't spook me. I just eyeballed him right back. I didn't act different, I chewed gum like a cow grindin' her stuff. It kinda calmed down my nerves. I stood there till the guard gave me a paper.

Fill this out, then put whatever you have in your pockets in this container.

"The cracker treated me like he was Superman, but I filled out the paper anyway. I gotta admit that my hand shook and I was havin' a hard time rememberin' my address and all the crap they already had. When I finished, Superman took the paper and handed it to another dude who acted like he was the big brain just 'cause he was workin' a goddamn comput-er. The prick gave me the slant-eye like I was scum, then clicked in somethin', pressed a button, and waited for the machine to spit out the paper. Superman looked at the thing and then real slow shuffled it back to me, actin' like he was the big kahoona.

Are you here to see Inmate Rosario Cota?

Yeah.

You're cleared. What do you have in your mouth?

Gum.

Over there's a tissue. Get rid of the gum. There's a wastebasket behind you.

"Dickhead! Who the hell did he think he was tellin' me to spit out the gum? When I got rid of the stuff I felt like shovin' the goddamn wad up his white ass, but I remembered that Sister Gladys tol' me not to make no waves with them bastards. They're junkyard dogs ready to rip the ass off anybody back-talkin'.

Walk through the electronic gate. Beyond it a guard will escort you to the visiting area. For your information, this inmate is coming from North Segregation. There's a fifteen to twenty minute wait.

"I started movin' to the gate, thinkin' that the guy was a real prick, when he yelled out. I turned around real slow and cool, lettin' him know that he wasn't nobody's daddy.

What's the inmate to you?

Mother.

Oh!

"That's all he said. Scumbag! Was it his goddamn business who Rosario was? He didn't say no more after that, maybe he guessed what I was thinkin'. He just waved his big paw tellin' me to get the hell outta there. He musta yelled out to prove he was controllin' me, but he wasn't. So I shuffled through the gate where Superman Number Two was waitin'. This time that scumbag was really packin'. He was wrapped up in a bulletproof vest and had a piece strapped to his waist. Not only that. He had a big stick in his hand, like he 'spected me to jump him any minute.

"I followed Superman down the ugly hallway. It didn't have no windows so it was real dark with only some washed-out gray lights to make sure some jerk didn't fall and break his goddamn neck. I blinked a lot till my eyeballs got used to the dark, but by that time we made it to wall-to-wall bars that stopped us. Superman pulled out his little walkie-talkie or whatever the hell it was he clicked on.

Visitor approaching guest area.

"One side of the bars slid open and Superman pushed me across the separation. As soon as we was on the other side, the damn bars wheeled shut behind us with a big bang. I took a look at the guy and after a while I knew that he looked more like Frankenstein than Superman. He never talked. He just breathed real loud like a burned-out gorilla.

"I followed Frankenstein around a corner till we got to a big cage where two more muscle-bound goons was holed up. Them crackers was loaded and packin' just like the other ones. One of the guys was standin' readin' somethin' and the other one was sittin'. When me and Frankenstein reached the cage, Sittin' Bull stood up and shoved some papers through a little door in the cage. I scoped out Sittin' Bull's mug. It was stiff-like a mask and even when the bugger talked his trap never even moved.

Sign this.

"I was so shaky by that time that I didn't even read what was on the shitty paper. I signed and to tell the truth my breathin' was gettin' all fucked up. I felt like my chest was fill-in' with rocks. Everythin' around me was comin' down on me so bad that I was scared of passin' out in one of my ol'-time fits. Suddenly, Sittin' Bull started talkin'.

Okay. You're cleared.

How long can I stay?

Let's see. It's a little past noon. You have until eating time. That gives you four hours.

Is that all?

"Sittin' Bull looked at me like I was a freak but he didn't gimme no answer. I caught how he looked at the other goon like they was havin' a big laugh on me.

Go over to that seat and wait for the inmate. It'll be fifteen or twenty minutes.

"I looked over to where he was pointin' and took in a chair pushed up against a table. I shuffled over to the place to see what it was all about and caught on right away. There was a phone hangin' on a wall on the side and a glass wall dividin' the table from the other side where there was another table and chair. I got real close to the glass. I wanted to see what else was on the other side but all I saw was a metal door that was shut tight.

"I knew right away what was goin' on. Rosario was gonna come outta that door, sit on the other side of the glass, and pick up her side of the phone. I sat down to wait and for sure the goddamn sweat started seepin' out all over me just thinkin' that this was the shitty way I was gonna meet her. This was my first time with her but I wouldn't be able to touch her or feel her touchin' me. Her voice wouldn't be her voice. It would be a fake wire voice.

"I started feelin' so goddamn sick that I laid my head on my arms, like I was sleepin', but what I was doin' was tryin' to knock down the big ball in my throat and the tears that was burnin' up my eyeballs. Then it suddenly hit me that I didn't want Rosario to see me like that, just a snivelin' dickhead. I hadda look good for her. That's why I'd gone to the store and bought some new pants and a snazzy sweater. I even got new sneakers and I gave myself a real close shave that morning. I did all that so Rosario would like me, so she wouldn't think I was some beat-up prick with snot runnin' down his nose. I straightened up and waited for her, tryin' to look cool even if my guts was curlin' inside me.

"Then the big door on the other side swung open and another Superman came through. The cracker was so big he nearly covered up the openin' but I caught a little bit of somebody walkin' behind him. I stood up and stretched my neck tryin' to see who it was but the jerk was too big, so I hadda wait till he moved to the side. Then I saw her. She stood there lookin' at me like she was seein' somethin' real strange. I looked back hopin' that I wouldn't pass out.

"Rosario and me eyeballed each other like we was caged buggers in a zoo. I took her in like my eyes was gonna swallow her up just lookin' at her shoulders, her eyes, her mouth. I stood up and got real close to the glass. I wanted to see her better. Rosario is tall and she's real beautiful but I hated the ugly red jumpsuit that hung on her like she was a dummy. I hated the big shoes even more.

"I don't know what I 'spected to see. Maybe a repeat of her pictures, maybe somethin' different. What I saw was that she was older, not a wrinkled up ol' bag, just older. She was skinny, like she didn't eat too much. When I looked hard at her it hit me that what others said was for real. I look like her, like Abuela always tol' me. Oh, God! I wanted so bad to jump over the glass and wrap myself around her! I hadda touch her but I couldn't, so I stood there gawkin' at her like I was some stupid moron.

"She stared at me, too, like she couldn't believe what she was lookin' at. Maybe she thought I was a ghost or somethin' like that, maybe even a circus freak. All I could tell was that she was stuck to the floor like she was nailed down. I didn't stop to remember that she was lookin' at me for the first time since that goddamn night, that now I was big and that my face looked like hers even if it did have a shadow on the jaw.

"I couldn't help myself but I slammed my hands flat on the glass, like that woulda got me closer to her and then I pasted my face to it. The glass fogged up quick, gettin' worse when my sweat got all over it, messin' it up somethin' awful. I forgot all about the phone but Rosario didn't, and when she picked up I did the same on my side.

Rafael.

"I can still hear her voice. I wanted to cry but I didn't want her to think I was a sissy even if holdin' it in made me feel shittier. I started to sweat all over even more and I could tell that the stuff was drippin' off my face, maybe even off my nose. I wiped it with my sleeve and made myself talk back.

Yeah.

"I could tell that Rosario was scared stiff like me and that she couldn't talk neither, so we looked at each other like a couple of dummies. Then a funny thing happened. It felt like we was talkin' without words, just with our eyes. I could tell that she heard me tellin' her that I was crazy happy just to look at her face, that I wanted to touch her and her to touch me. It's crazy, but my eyes went ahead and tol' her that I was a loner all my life, that I was a bum, a drunk, and even a dope head. She was seein' that I slept in alleys and in junkyards but that the only thing that kept me alive was thinkin' of her and that I never gave up on her. I knew she was innocent.

"She talked back with her eyes, too. She said that she was waitin' for me to come, that she wanted to see me but that she was scared. Them eyes tol' me how Abuela's letters tol' her all about me, that she sent pictures of me standin' by the tomato vines, on picnics, and in the house sittin' at the little table where I used to eat when I was with her.

"Then it stopped. The talkin' with our eyes, I mean, and we started to talk with our mouths, but it was stupid talk, nothin' important. We sounded like them morons who stand around burnin' time waitin' for the asshole bus to come.

How are you, Rafael?

Okay. How about you?

The same, thanks.

Where are you living?

Close to L.A.

Why so far?

Don't know. It just happened.

Do you go to school?

Nope. I have a job.

Oh? Doing what?

Packin' meat.

What kind of job is that?

It pays my room and food. Hey! How's the food here? It looks like you don't get enough to eat.

Food is food. I can take it or leave it.

"I didn't wanna keep on talkin' like a stupid idiot, so I clammed up, but I could feel her eyes cuttin' into me. Jesus! I wished I could come up with all the stuff I used to dream of tellin' her, but I sat there like a dickhead without a tongue. Nothin' came outta my trap. All the time I hung on to the phone like it was a rope and I was drownin' in mud. Finally, Rosario opened up.

Rafael, our time together is short and I don't know where to begin. I haven't been with you since you were a baby and I've seen you only in pictures Abuela sent me.

I look different.

Oh, yes! It's funny, but I kind of expected you to look like you did in those pictures when you were around ten or eleven. I wasn't ready for the grown-up man that you are.

Besides the pictures, did Abuela tell you about me?

Just about everything. She used to visit me a lot until she died and we talked mostly of you. What we didn't talk about she wrote in letters. She made sure I knew when you visited her in the summer and how the two of you went shopping and planted things in her garden. She told me the funny things that happened and how you always asked questions about me. She even let me know about the stories she told. After she died I missed her a lot because she was so important to me, but even more because when she left so did you. I lost track of you and how you grew up.

Does it make a difference? Did you want me to be a kid again?

Not exactly, but I wish I had been around to see you grow. I've missed out on a lot in life but the biggest loss was not being with you.

Yeah. I wished I coulda been with you, too. I used to make up games with you and me playin'. I talked to you and we invented neat things to do together.

Do you have a girlfriend?

Nope.

A good-looking guy like you?

"She caught me off guard with her screwy question so I shut up again. It felt like she was gettin' pretty close to askin' about my days on the streets when I used to jump bitches all the time. Honest to God, I felt ashamed that I didn't have no special girl to tell her about, someone to take to movies and crap like that, so I kept quiet.

Tell me about your father.

What do you wanna know?

Do you live with him?

Not anymore.

When did you last see him?

Not too long ago.

How does he look?

Ol'.

Does he live with anyone?

There's broads on and off. That's been goin' on since I was a kid.

Do you love him?

No.

Why not?

That's a screwy question! There's nothin' to love. I tried to whack him.

What?

Yeah. I tried to snuff him.

When?

Last time I saw him.

How?

With my hands. I woulda done it 'cept the maid conked me with a pan. The cops took me to jail but the ol' man dropped the charges.

I can't believe it.

Why not? He's a sonofabitch. Ain't that enough?

Rafael, I don't want to hear more about him. Let's talk about you. Tell me about yourself.

I just grew up, that's all. Like we already talked, I spent a lotta summers with Abuela but when she died I did different things. I wanted to see you mosta the time, but when I wrote you turned me down.

I remember.

Why?

Why what?

Why did you turn me down?

That's a long story, Rafael.

I wanna hear. We got time.

I don't want to go over it.

It was important to me. It hurt a lot.

I'm sorry but I couldn't help it.

I needed to be with you. You just said you missed seein' me grow. Why did you turn me down?

Rafael, I can't talk about it.

Abuela used to tell me about you when you was little.

Those days are gone.

I used to dream of you.

Let's talk of something else.

"I could tell that the both of us was gettin' pissed. Even her voice changed. I didn't wanna talk about myself and she didn't wanna talk about why she turned me down, so we both clammed up. We sat eyeballin' each other, wonderin' what would come up next. In a minute I decided I wanted to hear about the kids, so I took a chance hopin' that she wouldn't cork off.

Tell me about the kids.

What about them?

Goddamn it! How did they act? What did they look like? How did they talk?

Not with a bad mouth like yours!

Do people around here talk like angels?

If you keep this up, I'm out of here!

Okay! Okay! Just tell me somethin' about the kids. Please!

They were little. They were precious. They were adorable.

Do you miss them?

Rafael, I can't go on with this!

Do you miss me?

What do you think? You're my baby.

Then why didn't you let me come see you?

I'm leaving!

No! Wait! I wanna tell you what I done to prove that you didn't do it.

What?

Yeah! I even took a bus down to Mexico.

What for?

I tracked down your maid. Candelaria Fontes. Remember her?

You talked to her?

Yeah!

How? Do you speak Spanish?

A little, but she talks plenty English.

How did you find her?

I snooped around here and there till I came up with the place where she lives. Abuela used to talk about her.

What did Candelaria say?

A lotta things about you and the ol' man.

Like what?

That she watched you guys over the years and saw how he stepped out on you.

That's not important anymore, Rafael.

It's important to me. It tells me that he was the same asshole with you like he was with me.

What else did she say?

That you guys boozed and got into it all kinds of times.

Yes, we did that. What else?

She says she don't know who killed the kids.

I don't want to talk about this anymore, Rafael. Anyway, it's time for me to leave.

Don't we have more time?

No. I've got to go. Will you come tomorrow?

Yeah. The permit says I got two meetings with you. Can I bring you somethin'?

I don't care. Maybe a magazine.

"I stood up and watched her walk away from me till the big door swallowed her. Then I shuffled over to Sittin' Bull and tol' him to let me out. He took me to the main gate, all the time me feelin' like crap 'cause I didn't tell Rosario what was inside me. I didn't say that I knew she was innocent, that one day she would come home with me. But that wasn't all I was feelin'. I was all mixed up, too. I couldn't figure out why she went away when we still had time left on the clock. She made me feel that she didn't wanna be with me no more and I couldn't understand it. Was I such a big asshole? Was I so goddamn ugly that she couldn't stand me?

"Sister Gladys was waitin' for me in her jalopy when I walked out to the parking lot. I jumped in but she didn't say nothin' till we rolled up to the front of the motel.

They have a pretty good pizza around the corner. I'll get one and meet you in your room.

No, thanks. I ain't hungry.

I know, but you're going to eat anyway. I'll see you in a few minutes.

"I sat in the room thinkin' real hard till she came back with the pizza. I didn't wanna eat but I did and while we ate I tol' her about what happened with Rosario. Sister Gladys let me talk and talk. She was one big ear, like she knew what was inside me and she didn't have to ask no stupid questions. She knew that I hadda spit the whole thing out before I blew up like I was a goddamn balloon. Then, after she went to her room, I crashed on the bed till the next morning when she rapped on the door."

CHAPTER 19

"The second time went faster once I got through the big gate. It was a different buncha guys up front this time. I guess they had all the paperwork they needed so nobody asked no stupid questions. The big dude at the desk just gave me the box for the stuff in my pockets and then pointed to the metal gate. I walked down the hall with the other asshole more easy this time till I saw Sittin' Bull by his desk. He gave me the eagle eye and I gave it right back.

"When Rosario showed up I was feelin' cool 'cause I knew what I was gonna say this time. I was gonna watch it, not come out with nothin' to cork her off. I didn't want her to kick me out again even if I didn't get her the fuckin' magazine.

"She came outta the metal door lookin' better, like she slept good that night. I was glad. I didn't want us to get into it again. I had too much inside me that I wanted her to hear.

Hello, Rafael.

Hi.

Are you feeling okay?

Yeah. Why? Do I look crappy?

No. You look better today.

I forgot the magazine.

That's okay. I forgot about it myself. Rafael, we only have a short time and I want to tell you some things. Yesterday you asked me to talk about the kids and I'm sorry I didn't. I guess you caught me by surprise.

Can you talk today?

Yes. Your brother and sisters were just everyday kids, yet they were real special; each one had something different. We did a lot of things together, stuff like other families.

Like what?

*We went on picnics and hiking and we played games togeth-
er.*

Did the ol' man do it too?

*Yes. We did most things together. The big deal was on days
like Christmas and Thanksgiving. Birthdays were special.*

*Abuela told me that you guys got into it all the time. Even
Candelaria Fontes said the same thing.*

It's no use talking about that.

I wanna know.

*Okay. We argued a lot. I think it was because we drank too
much and got drunk lots of the time.*

Then what?

What do you mean?

What did you fight about?

Married people stuff.

Like what?

*Little things, like why he was late for a meal or why he didn't
sleep at home on a couple of nights.*

That ain't little. Was he sleeping around?

Yes.

*Same ol' sonofabitch. Why didn't you kick him in the ass?
Tell him to hit the road?*

*It's not that easy. One day when you're married you'll
understand.*

I ain't never gonna marry.

Maybe.

Did you guys ever beat up on each other?

Yes.

Did you kick the shit outta him?

Sometimes. Other times he beat me up.

Did you think of leavin' him?

*Yes. That was the big argument that night, except it wasn't
me that was asking for the divorce. He's the one that had the
papers all made out.*

What's the difference? Why didn't you just walk out on him?

I couldn't.

What about me? Where was I all that time?

You were there, too, once you came along.

If I was part of it, why did you turn me down when I wanted to see you? It woulda made a big difference to me.

It wasn't because I didn't love you.

Is it 'cause I was left alive?

What? What do you mean?

I mean that the other kids, the good ones, were snuffed out and a shit like me was left alive.

How can you talk that way? You were just as special, maybe even more than the others.

Then why did you shut me off?

I was nervous, scared.

Scared of me? Why?

You can't understand but I'll say it anyway. I thought that for sure you hated me and I knew I couldn't take it. I told you yesterday. You're my baby. A mother can't stand being hated by her child. You're the last, the only one in the world that I love.

Why would I hate you?

Why? I'm in prison because they say I killed your brother and sisters. Isn't that a reason to be hated?

Yeah, if I believed it.

You don't believe it?

No! You didn't kill them. Did you?

No! I mean, I don't remember.

You didn't do it! I know it! Just tell me that you didn't do it and that's what I'll believe. Tell me! Now! Tell me what happened!

Rafael, I don't remember.

What's that mean? Did you or didn't you do it?

I'm telling you I don't remember!

Goddamn it! You gotta remember somethin'! There's gotta be some little thing left that you remember. How about me? I was just a twerp. Am I part of what you forgot?

You're all I ever thought of. I thought a lot of the other kids, too, but most of all you. It's that night that I can't remember even though I've spent all these years trying.

How come that lame lawyer of yours didn't bring this up to the goddamn jury?

He did his best.

What about the cops? They was so pushed and in a hurry to nail somebody down. They never did no tests or nothin' like that to prove it wasn't you.

Maybe. Yet, everything points to it.

Points to what? What everythin' are you talkin' about?

The evidence.

Evidence? That's bullshit! It was all fixed.

If I didn't do it, then who did it?

"Rosario's voice got real soft, makin' me shove the telephone so hard against my ear that it started to hurt real bad. I could tell that she was gettin' ready to come off the wall with some bullshit rag that maybe it was her who done it and I didn't wanna hear that kinda crap. I felt my belly gettin' all messed up, scared that she was cavin' in, that she was ready to fess up to what she never done.

You didn't do it!

I don't remember.

Goddamn it! You didn't do it.

Rafael, I want you to listen to me like you've never listened to anybody in your life. I've been waiting around for a long time, for years, and I've hoped that something would come up to prove what I wanted the most, but nothing ever happened. I've lived in stinking tiny cells, nearly losing my mind from loneliness and shattered hopes. I've thought and thought, always trying to remember, but I can't. There's only a black hole and I can't get anything out of it.

You didn't do it!

Rafael, calm down!

You wanna drive me crazy?

No! It's the other way around! If you don't calm down you'll drive yourself crazy. Listen to me! I'm going to tell you what I've never told anybody. No matter how much I tried, I just couldn't make my life work when I was with your father. I admit it. I screwed up so bad that all I got out of life was empty hands and a blank memory. I loved the kids and I wanted to keep them, but they dripped through my fingers like water.

Why are you takin' all the blame? What about the ol' man?

Him, too. Maybe it was the both of us, but I think it was mostly me. Now I'm tired, so tired and I don't want to go on. I'm tired of never seeing the sun rise or set, of never sitting by the beach the way I used to. Most of all, I'm sick and tired of not being with you or with your brother and sisters. I eat my heart out for missing out on all those lost years, months and months of not being with the four of you. If I killed those children, then it's for sure that I've paid for what I might've done by being caged up so long. Now I want to be free but I know that the only way is through the chamber.

You didn't do it!

I want you to know that I'm at peace. I made up with God a long time ago when I prayed and thought about what I might've done. I saw that I wasn't the only sinner, that bigger sins have been committed. I looked at the Magdalene, how she was almost stoned to death, but she was forgiven. Just like her I talk to God all the time and I know that I'm forgiven. I know it here in my heart. I'm going to join the kids soon, but I'll be back to be with you. I promise.

Rosario, I can't breathe!

Let go of me, Rafael! Please let go!

"I don't remember nothin' after she said them words. Everythin' went black. It was like some monster thing came and shoved me into a pit, a hole so deep that it didn't have no bottom and I fell into it with my head danglin' straight down. I went into the black mud even when I tried to grab somethin', but there wasn't nothin'. My fingers scratched and yanked, tryin' to stop me from drownin' in the shit that was coverin' me.

"The next thing I remember hearin' was cryin' so bad that I thought maybe somebody chopped off the poor guy's leg. It was a down deep bawlin' that reminded me of when I was a brat yelling out for Rosario. Little by little I started crawlin' outta the shit where I fell. I seen that I was on my ass spread out against a wall and that it was me who was cryin' like a baby. Sittin' Bull was by my side and he was on his ass too.

Hey, Kid! You okay?

What happened?

You passed out. Here're some tissues. Wipe your face.

I gotta see her!

She's gone.

Lemme see her!

I told you she's gone. Now get on your feet because you're outta here right now!

"I gawked at the guy like I'd lost my marbles. I did it till he took me by the arms and hauled me back on my feet. He gave me a few minutes to get my shit together and then we shuffled away from the cage, away from where Rosario musta gone. I moved like a zombie that don't hear nothin', not even the goddamn bars clankin' made a difference. I didn't give a shit about the walls or the floor or nothin'. I don't even remember how long it took to cross the gates or how I made it to the parking lot to Sister Gladys and her jalopy.

"When we hit the road we didn't say nothin' about what happened between me and Rosario, but I knew that Gladys was caught up on everythin'. Them little eyes don't miss nothin'. She saw my sweater all wet with tears and snot and slime. She saw my bloated mug and red eyeballs, but she didn't say nothin' till we got to the motel.

Rafael, let me spend the night in your room. I can sleep in the easy chair. I've done it many times in my life.

No, Sister. I wanna be by myself.

Okay. I understand but do me a big favor. Please leave your door unlocked. Will you do that for me? I'll be honest with you. I'll be peeking in during the night.

Yeah. I don't care.

"She went away and after that the next thing I remember is that I was on my knees in front of the toilet bowl. I was pukin' and slobberin', nearly chokin' on the crap my belly was shovin' up through my mouth and nose. I was bawlin' so bad that my body kept heavin' against the bowl, makin' my ribs hurt like hell.

"When that stopped I fell back on my ass and I seen that this was the end of the road for me. I came all the way from bein' a kid spooked by dreams, pissin' on the bed every night. It was the same road that took me to the streets of L.A. and from there on the hunt for assholes to tell me the truth. I even tried to whack the ol' man on that fuckin' road. It pulled me to Rosario where I saw her face to face and where she nearly did me in by tellin' me to let go of her.

"All my life I waited just to meet her. All that time I hung on for that one minute, but that minute came and went and I couldn't figure out what the hell it was all about. What did it mean? It was like I waited all my life for the bus that was gonna take me to Rosario but it turned out to be nothin' but a bus outta control. When it came it passed me up, leaving me behind with nothin' in my hands. Was this all there was to it? Was this all there was to my whole goddamn life? One stinkin' empty minute?

"I got off my ass, crawled to the bed, and flopped into it. I was too beat up to do anythin' else so I stayed there starin' at the ceiling, thinkin' about what Rosario said. I couldn't make out what the hell she meant when she said she was forgiven. For what? She ain't guilty of nothin'! Why did she have to come up with all that bullshit talk about Magdalene, whoever the hell she was. I never even heard of her. I caught on that Rosario was tryin' to tell me that maybe she whacked the kids but she didn't fool me. I knew that she was just puttin' me on, tryin' to make me back off. I was sure that she didn't mean what she was sayin'.

"I tried to sleep but my head was stuffed, all churned up. For a long time I thought I heard the goddamn voices. Most of all, I couldn't get rid of the pictures of Rosario sittin' on the other side of the glass wall and her voice tellin' me that she was comin' back. This happened over and over all night long. Inside me her words was eatin' me up, but I still didn't swallow her story. I just couldn't."

CHAPTER 20

"The next morning I climbed into the car with Sister Gladys who still didn't ask me nothin' about what happened between me and Rosario. I knew that she kept lookin' into my room all night. I guess she figured that maybe I'd try some kinda monkey business. That was cool with me. I knew she was doin' that 'cause she was worried about me.

"We rolled outta the parking lot and she pointed the jalopy toward Los Angeles on 101, and once we was on the road that foot of hers pushed down hard on the gas, leavin' Quentin behind us. All the time I kept thinkin' of the monster cement walls trappin' Rosario, Sittin' Bull, and all the supermen that ran the place.

"I don't know how long we was on the road. All I remember is that the ocean disappeared, hills came outta nowhere, and all the time the night without sleep started to catch up on me. I was feelin' bum, like my belly was all tied up, on fire, and my head was close to explodin'. I wanted to cough up what happened to Sister Gladys but I couldn't. The words just wouldn't come outta my trap. Finally, Gladys opened up.

Are you hungry?

No.

Well, I'd like a cup of coffee and a sandwich. We're close to Paso Robles. I remember a roadside diner just south of town where we can stop. I hope the place still exists.

"I didn't care what we did. I shook my shoulders, tellin' her that whatever she wanted was cool with me, but I still didn't talk. My guts was kickin' up more now and I didn't want no food. For sure I would puke all over the jalopy. I don't know if it was the churnin' in my belly, or maybe it was the poundin' goin' on in my head but I started seein' Rosario all over again. I just couldn't push that picture away no matter how much I tried. I saw her flat on her back on the stretcher with her legs and arms tied down. Her face was jerkin' sideways, eyeballin' the vultures gawkin' through the window, and she could see that the scumbags could hardly wait for her to start croakin'.

"Then those shitheads got all mixed up with a picture of her sittin' in a cell, like the one I saw in them pictures I seen. Her head hung into her hands and I knew she was decidin' between the stinkin' needle and the poison gas. All this happened that night when I tried to sleep, but now in the car her voice came back to me louder. It was makin' my head pound like a drum.

Shit!

What's the matter?

My head's gonna explode.

You didn't sleep, that's why. Hang on. I'll give you an aspirin as soon as we make it to the diner.

I slept all right. I don't have no problem.

"That Sister Gladys! I lied but she's always hip to what's goin' on inside me. She guessed right. I didn't get no sleep 'cept for a few minutes when I drifted off and that didn't help. I kept snappin' outta it thinkin' I caught the ol' voices hangin' around the bed. They had backed off for a long time so when I heard them I was so surprised that I sprang up in the bed and looked around for them little assholes. I tol' myself that if I nailed them in the cemetery I could catch them again. But I was wrong. I didn't see no ugly, squirmin' sonsabitches this time. When I tried to get some sleep after that, pictures of Rosario came back all over the place inside my head.

We're in luck. The diner is still there.

"Sister Gladys pulled into a parking spot, slammed on the brakes, and jumped outta the jalopy without sayin' nothin'. I followed her. The place was a greasy spoon with a long counter on one side and a few booths pushed up against a big window on the other side. It was stuffed with a buncha bums, but there was one empty table so we headed straight for it and waited for the waitress to come.

Howdy, folks. Here's the menu. I'll tell you that our special is pretty good. It's a tuna salad sandwich with lentil soup. Comes with potato chips.

I'll take the sandwich and soup.

Anything to drink?

Ice tea.

Sir? What about you?

Nothin'.

Rafael, take the soup. It'll help settle your stomach.

My stomach's okay.

I'll bring you a cup of soup. It's pretty tasty.

"I could tell that Sister Gladys wanted me to eat somethin'; she was gettin' bent outta shape just lookin' at me. It looked like she was waitin' to ask what happened between me and Rosario but was a little shaky about it. Maybe she was waitin' for the right minute or maybe she 'spected me to cough it up when I was ready, but now she was gettin' nervous. She saw me gettin' all messed up, right there in fronta her.

"She couldn't tell half of it 'cause I was sinkin' into a deep hole real fast, even if I was fightin' it. Still, I was glad that she wasn't needlin' me about what happened with Rosario. I was gonna tell her anyway, I just needed more time. On the other hand, thinkin' back maybe it woulda helped to open up right there and then.

"I tried to think of somethin' else so I started lookin' around, just watchin' people. They was havin' a good time, scarfin' up burgers and cokes and I was feelin' a little bit better till I caught some of them scumbags eyeballin' me. At first I thought I made a mistake but then I looked real hard to make sure I was right. It wasn't no mistake! Them assholes was havin' a ball just gawkin' at me, whisperin' behind dirty hands coverin' their goddamn traps. They was tryin' to cover up what they was sayin' about me but they didn't fool me. Some of them bastards was even makin' noises about me. I turned real quick and caught some ol' bag gawkin' at me with pig eyes and I could tell how much she hated my guts.

"Those pig eyes scared me, so I turned to look out the window. I couldn't stand lookin' at the ol' bag no more but after a while I hadda look back. When I did it I saw that I done a mistake in the first place. All them people was mindin' their ever-loving business. They wasn't lookin' at me after all. I thought I was losin' my marbles, so I rubbed my eyes and took another look and I saw that it wasn't no trick. People was eatin' and yakkin' normal, just sittin' in their chairs.

"I was sweatin' so much that my shirt stuck to my back, makin' me know somethin' was crankin' me on, somethin' awful. I looked at Sister Gladys, but she was readin' a leftover newspaper. I wanted to tell her how bad I was feelin' but my tongue was stiff like a stick and I just couldn't talk. The only thing I could think of doin' was to eyeball all them people again to make sure I was wrong in the first place.

"Goddamn it! When I looked again I saw that I was right all along! Them assholes was out to get me! They was gonna make dog meat outta me for sure! I couldn't tell what they was mumblin' but I heard them say my name and it wasn't one or two of 'em either. It was all of 'em that was doin' it.

"Then I caught three scumbags tryin' to hide behind a menu but I seen enough to catch that they was the super guards from the pen. Them slimebags thought I didn't remember them. How could I forget them ugly mugs! I even caught how their hands was reachin' for their pieces, fingers already on the trigger. I tightened up, waitin' to be plugged right there in front of the sister. I knew that them assholes hated me big-time but that was okay with me. I hated their guts just as much. Besides, I knew that I shoulda been snuffed out a long time ago anyway. It was time to get it over.

Hey, Fucker! How's about a bowl of donkey piss?
What?

"When I answered the voice, Sister Gladys's face snapped up and she stared at me like I had two dicks growin' outta my head. I think I spooked her real bad. Then she turned around to see if somebody in back of her was talkin' to me. When she didn't see nobody she looked back at me.

I didn't say anything, Rafael.
I thought you said somethin'.
Rafael, are you all right?
Yeah. I'm okay. Why?
You're very pale. Here. Take a drink of water.

"I swear the voice I heard was real clear. For a second I thought maybe it was some customer sittin' close, but in a second I knew. Oh, yeah, I knew that it was one of the little shitheads talkin'! I gawked at Sister Gladys so hard that she started to wiggle around, gettin' real nervous, and she kept lookin' at the kitchen door like she couldn't wait for the food to come.

Go ahead and drink the fucking water, you stinking shit-head! You did it again, didn't you? Now even your ol' lady is gonna fry. When is it gonna be your turn?

"I shut my eyes tight. I knew that them turds finally nailed me. They danced around my bed the night before but backed off just to make me think I was dreamin'. Now I saw that they was plannin' to play a game with me. They knew I was wiped out and couldn't fight back, 'specially in front of Sister Gladys and all them other people.

Hey asshole! Thought you had it down pat, didn't you? Look at you, all nervous and sweaty, just like any broken-down god-damned piece of shit.

"I knew I didn't stand a chance with 'em, so I jumped up ready to get outta the place but Sister Gladys grabbed my arm. I flopped back into the chair. I just couldn't push back. She was stronger than me.

Ooooooh! Little dickhead Ralphie! What's wrong with you, dog turd? How come you're not so tough with the wrinkled ol' broad like you was with your ol' man? Why not twist her chicken neck, too? It's easy! Come on! Do it!

"I yanked my arm from Sister's fingers and tried to get away from her. I couldn't stand it! My lungs was chokin' me. I couldn't breathe, so my legs pushed me away from the table, tryin' to get me to some air. Then my brain went crazy tellin' me to jump somebody, to come down on any one of them scumbags real fast.

"I couldn't help it but my head kept turnin' around like a stupid ball, eyeballin' the stinkin' tables and takin' in everybody in the packed place. That's when I saw them pricks givin' me the finger. I shifted my eyes down to Sister Gladys and saw that she was sittin' stiff, gawkin' at me like she knew that I was gonna grab some slime's neck real quick.

Go ahead, sonofabitch. Attack! Attack! Maybe some fucker will bring you down and pack you into a goddamn coffin. You're just a piece of horseshit anyway!

Shut up!

"I heard myself screamin' and I caught how everybody almost jumped outta their chairs 'cause my yellin' spooked them. They stopped talkin' and even the bullshit music comin' outta the walls stopped. Outta the side of my eye I saw a couple of dudes stand up ready to jump me. Sister Gladys did the same thing. She wanted to reach me, to drag me outta the place but it was too late. I lost it.

"My head was explodin' and red dots was flyin' all over the place in fronta my eyes. I couldn't help it but my fingers got all fucked up. They was squirmin' like a buncha stinkin' worms even when I tried to keep them straight. I got scared outta my gourd when I felt my chest crackin' open with all the screams I kept hearin'.

Ralphie, you motherfucker! Move! Quick! Do something! Jump all over the fuckers before they get you!

"The howlin' in my head kept gettin' louder and even if Sister Gladys was quick, I was faster. This time I jerked away from her and made it across the room headin' for the counter. I jumped over the thing like my feet had wings and not one of them shitheads sittin' at the tables stood a chance to block me. When I landed, I shoved the waitress on her ass and then I ran down the damn counter scrapin' off all them dishes and glasses with my arms that was like stiff rods.

"Everythin' went flyin'. Bottles, shakers, plates with chewed up burgers, forks, knives, napkins; every goddamn thing went off the counter like they had wings. They crashed on the floor and splattered garbage all over them freaked out assholes that was so spooked they couldn't do jackshit to stop me.

"The racket from my yellin' was so big that even them mean honchos that gave me the finger was scared outta their gourds and they didn't do nothin' but gawk at me with their traps hangin' open. And me? I attacked and attacked like everythin' was frozen stiff and I hadda melt it down all by myself. Sister Gladys tol' me afterward that no one could tell the cops nothin' about when it started or even how long it took me to trash the goddamn place. Nobody knew nothin' 'cept that I messed up their day real bad.

"After that I don't remember nothin', 'cept that when I woke up I was tied down like a hog. My arms was pasted hard on my chest, even my feet was strapped down, and my eyelids and lips felt like balloons. I kind a figured out that I was on a stretcher, maybe in a van. I was movin' from one side to the other. I didn't know where the hell I was goin' or even what happened to Sister Gladys.

"I remembered the diner up to when I got all pissed with what the buggers was squealin' in my ears. After that things went blank. Now I wanted to talk, to yell out, but my tongue was a stiff ball. Only my ears was still workin' and I could hear some morons talkin'. I caught on that they was yappin' about me.

Christ! This one's a winner, ain't he? It took five guys to put him down. I never had one that kicked and thrashed so hard. He was even biting like a goddamn wild dog. He'll be in that jacket for a long time.

Did you see the mess he made of the diner? I wouldn't want to pay that bill.

It'll have to be the insurance, that's for sure. This bugger ain't gonna come up with much money real soon.

"I forced my puffed-up eyes to open and I saw two jerks sittin' next to me. Even in the dark I could tell they was dressed in white and that there was different kinds of gear all over the place. I closed my eyes and tried again to remember, but all that came back to me was a lotta ass kickin' and cussin'. I remembered when the big needle came down on me. I felt that part even when the thing came from somewhere behind me. After that I gave up tryin' to remember and I floated into a black pit while the two assholes kept yakkin'.

"Sometime after that I snapped outta that black pit. I didn't know what day or time it was and all I knew was that them goons was jerkin' the stretcher off the van. They didn't give a damn how they did it or that it hurt like hell each time they shoved the goddamn thing. The only thing I could hear was a lotta gruntin', cussin', and doors slammin' in my ears. Some asshole was askin' questions but nobody knew jackshit about what happened. I didn't care 'cause I was hurtin' so much. Then somethin' like a buncha years went by before I made out Sister Gladys's voice.

Rafael, you'll be here for a while. You're not alone. I'll stay as long as it takes. Don't resist and you'll be safe."

CHAPTER 21

Rafael finished telling his story. Elena was listening to him but her eyes were riveted somewhere beyond the window; she was looking toward the trees. The rain had stopped and a soft glow covered the garden and the windowpanes. Inside, muffled sounds swirled around them: murmurs, clicking billiard balls, shuffling of patients from one side of the room to the other.

"Well, that's the end of the road for now. The wheel that started spinnin' when I set out to prove that Rosario is innocent went crazy till it spun outta control in the diner; right there, in fronta everybody. It landed me flat on my ass in the crazy house in Atascadero. In case you don't know, that's the place that takes in only big-time killer nuts, the kind that go around slittin' throats and even eatin' arms and livers after they make the kill.

"After the big needle put me down that day, I drifted in and outta clouds. I didn't know where the hell I was or that I was wrapped in a jacket that pinned down my arms. I didn't even know that only my legs and ankles wasn't tied down. I just couldn't feel nothin' in my body. I was punchy all the time and I seen nothin' but shadows; everythin' was in slow motion. It took a long time before I caught on that I was on a bed propped up against the wall, just like a bag of potatoes. The place was little, with only one window, and when I saw a metal door I figured I wasn't going no place fast. I was in a trap.

"I don't know how long I was there; maybe it was days, maybe months. All I remember is that I couldn't think. My brain was broken down by all the shit that was pumped into my arm not once but a lotta times. I drifted through black clouds, feelin' a buncha people around me. I even heard voices, not the little creeps from before, just morons mutterin' about this or that bullshit. Almost always a strong wind sucked me up where I hung in the middle of nothin', twistin' me first in one direction, then in another one.

"It wasn't bad and my body relaxed. I kindda liked the feelin' and didn't put up no fight. I just gave in to the rockin' back and forth feelin' real good. It was like I was a bird hangin' from nothing. Like I had monster wings that kept me up in the middle of the air where nothin' was gonna come down on me or scare the hell outta me.

"That crap stopped when the shrinks decided to get started pickin' my brain but that's about the time when Sister Gladys stepped in and saved my ass. She made 'em understand that I wasn't no lunatic like the rest of them locked up degenerates. It took a lotta talkin' for her to get 'em to see what she was all about, but she done it. After a few days, or maybe it was weeks, she got me sprung and I landed here where I been talkin' to you."

Elena leaned over and turned off the recorder. It had now grown quiet in the room; she and Rafael were alone. She sighed, knowing that what had begun as an interview had now ended and she admitted that she was not sure of what next to say or do. She knew, however, that for the time being there were still some loose ends; she decided to bring them up.

"Rafael, what about the dreams you told me about in the beginning? Do they still bother you?"

"Nope! All gone."

"Really?"

"Well, what I mean is, the second one is gone. The one with the gun and my stretched out neck disappeared. The big one, the one where I almost see who done the killin' won't go away. It comes in the night."

"I thought you said the pills helped you through the night."

"Yeah, but it comes when I'm sleepin'. Maybe the thing will fade away after I make out the shadow. One day I'm gonna see who pulled the trigger and when that happens everythin' will change."

"It's a dream, Rafael. Let go of it."

"Maybe."

"What about the voices that came in the cemetery and diner?"

"Nope! Them little turds hit the road once I did what they tol' me to do."

"In the diner?"

"Yeah."

"What's going to happen the next time you do what they want you to do?"

"Are you puttin' me on? They wasn't for real. Now I know they was my voice talkin' to me. They was nothin', just me eatin' my heart out. They're not comin' back, that's for sure."

"I'm glad to hear you say it. Now, let me ask you about Sister Gladys."

"What about her?"

"Where is she? Does she visit you? She did a lot for you."

"She saved my ass, that's for sure, but she don't visit me no more. Her bosses shipped her off to New Mexico."

"New Mexico? Why?"

"She's a sister and she hits the road when she gets her marchin' papers."

"I forgot. That makes sense but does she keep in touch with you?"

"All the time. She writes a lotta letters filled with 'Do this! Do that! Don't fight, Rafael!' She's somethin' else, that little bugger."

"Do you write to her?"

"Oh, yeah, all the time. I even tol' her about you and she keeps askin' me all kinds of questions."

"About me?"

"Yeah."

"I'd like to meet her."

"Why?"

"Well, hearin' you talk about her makes me feel I almost know her. I want to meet her in person."

"I don't think that's gonna happen."

"We'll see, Rafael. It could happen. What about your father?"

"What kind of joke is that?"

"No, I'm serious."

"I ain't seen him since the jailhouse."

They dropped off into a long silence after this exchange. It had begun to rain again and the patter against the windows was the only sound that broke their silence. Elena felt exhaustion overcoming her but since she did not know when they would meet again, she tried to shake off her fatigue. There was yet another loose end that she wanted to bring up but she was apprehensive, knowing that it was the most sensitive point with Rafael. After a few moments of reflection, she made the decision.

"I'd like to ask you more about your mother."

"I thought so."

"Did you? Good, because I don't want you to get angry at me."

"Go for it!"

"All along you've insisted that your mother is innocent, but in our latest meetings I sense a change in you. Am I right?"

"No! You're wrong! She ain't guilty and I ain't never changed my mind about it."

"Rafael, didn't she let you understand that she did it? Did I hear it all wrong?"

"Yeah! You heard it all wrong! What she said was that she screwed up her life and that she let the kids drip through her fingers. That's not sayin' that she whacked them."

"Rafael, she asked you to let go of her!"

"Yeah, and I nearly lost my marbles on account of that shit!"

"Then I see that I'm really wrong."

"'About what?"

"I was beginning to think that you were letting go of her. I thought that after your experiences in Atascadero and here, you finally understood her wanting to be free, but now your anger tells me that I'm completely wrong."

"I ain't mad. I just got a little excited."

"Rafael, how are you going to deal with this for the rest of your life? Have you thought of that?"

"Look. She's innocent and I'm gonna prove it. I know it's gonna take a buncha years, only next time around I ain't gonna be a jerk again. I'm gonna go out there and learn the ropes, learn how to talk and think right, get money to bring on a fast-talking, know-it-all lawyer, and together we're gonna prove the real thing. I know it'll be too late to save Rosario but we'll make them cops, lawyers, judge, and jury fess up that they didn't do the job right the first time around. They're gonna have to face the monster mistake they made and then it's them who's gonna eat their hearts out."

Elena looked at Rafael, trying to understand him. Was he a fool? Was he so obsessed that he could not get hold of a reality that told him that his mother was guilty? Why did he so stubbornly cling to the impossibility of proving her innocence?

Absorbed by these questions, Elena was suddenly distracted when she saw that he had leaned back into the chair and covered his face with both hands. She saw that his chest was heaving and for a brief moment she was afraid of another outburst. However, her apprehension passed quickly because she understood that what he was expressing was not rage but the painful determination to follow through on what he had begun. After a while he dropped his hands, showing that tears had slipped out of his eyes.

"What I wanna believe is that before I can do what I gotta do, I first have to find the life my sisters and brother missed, a good life, not a messed up thing goin' from nuthouse to nuthouse. But when I start thinkin' this way, I ask if a bum like me can pull that off. Can I live like other people? Jesus! Thinkin' this way spooks the hell outta me."

"Why?"

"I never been like other people, that's why. I been a freak all my life, a miserable scumbag."

"Those words aren't yours, Rafael. They're the nasty voices talking again. You just said that they've gone away, but now I've heard them myself. They're talking through your mouth, using your tongue."

His eyes clung to her face and he appeared to be holding his breath; his brow wrinkled, radically changing his expression. Elena was now sitting on the edge of her chair, anxious about what he might say or do. They stared at one another for a while until he relaxed back into the chair and spoke softly.

"You think I can live like other people?"

"I do."

"Maybe. It's real tricky. I don't know how my brain is gonna act up next. What I do know is that I don't want all this pain no more. Like Rosario, I wanna be free."

"I think you're already free."

"What? What did you say?"

Elena did not answer Rafael. She was too drained, but as she gazed at him she realized that she was convinced that he was indeed free. Something had happened to change him since her first encounters with him. Perhaps it had been the medication or the doctor's therapy or even Sister Gladys's strong presence in his life. Or could it have been, Elena asked herself, Rafael's re-living his story.

This thought linked her mind to another question: How would he cope with the death of Rosario Cota when the time came for her execution? Elena could not summon the courage to pose that question, so she decided that only time would provide the answer. It was a cowardly decision, she knew, but she simply did not have the strength to ask the question. Suddenly, Rafael's question moved her away from her thoughts.

"Are you gonna write my story?"

"In time."

"You can say anythin' you want about me. You can even cut out my crappy talk."

"I'll think about it."

"So what's next?"

"I'm not sure."

"I guess you won't come back."

"Yes, I will. I'm sure there'll be a ton of questions that will come up."

They fell into an awkward silence, as if both wanted to speak but neither knew what to say. Elena, for the first time, had run out of questions and Rafael showed that he did not want her to leave. She finally broke the ice.

"I just got an idea, Rafael. How'd you like for us to drive to New Mexico? I want to meet Sister Gladys and I think you'd like to see those big-time deserts and rock formations."

"What?"

"Yes! A little trip."

"You seen that part of the country?"

"I have family in Santa Fe."

"Well, I don't know."

"What don't you know?"

"I don't think the shrinks'll let me outta here."

"Of course they will! The director keeps telling me of your improvement. Sure! Why not?"

"Hold on! Take it easy!"

"Why?"

"I gotta think about it."

"Are you afraid?"

"Me? Chicken? You're kiddin'!"

"Okay! Leave it up to me."

"Maybe we oughta think more about it."

"What for? It's a good idea."

They had gotten to their feet and stood looking at one another as if for the first time, but Elena, exited by the new idea, missed the look of anxiety that had crept into Rafael's eyes. All she was thinking was that she wanted to put her arms around him to comfort him, to let him know that he could be loved, that he could be free; that he would find what he was looking for. She wanted to do that, but she did not.

"Good-bye, Rafael. I'll come over for Christmas, if it's okay with you. It's only a few days from now."

"Oh, yeah, that's cool. But what about your family?"

"I'll spend Christmas Eve with them."

She took her things, walked a short way, and then looked back. She saw that he was partly turned away from her but looking at her through the corner of his eye. She left the room and headed for her car, thinking that he was saying good-bye with his Indio slant-eye look, as he liked to say.

CHAPTER 22

Elena sat in her car waiting for the green light. It would be a while before she could make it to the intersection since it was a five-way signal and she was caught in backed-up Christmas traffic. She waited patiently, hardly thinking of the delay, mostly because her thoughts were still with Rafael. The rain had not let up and the clicking of the wipers gave a back-and-forth rhythm to her thoughts.

The pleased mood she had experienced when saying good-bye to Rafael was fading. Part of what she was feeling was bewilderment that she had invited him to take the trip to New Mexico. She had not planned to drive anywhere with him, so she was baffled as to what had prompted the idea. However, it had happened and she was glad now that it had taken shape. Why not? It would be a good time to get to know him better. These thoughts settled her jittery nerves somewhat and she returned her attention to the sluggish traffic. She had moved her car forward a few feet but the jam was mostly at a standstill.

Elena looked out the side window and saw that she was in front of a crowded shopping mall. Through the rain, she made out gleaming oversized signs: Nordstrom's, Rite Aide, Robinson-May, Penney's. Then she focused on the milling crowds, some struggling with umbrellas, others hooded against the downpour, most of them with packages and bags in hand as they made their way in and out of stores or standing at crossways waiting for walk signs. Everywhere she looked there was color from decorated windows and trees dripping with twinkling lights. She stretched to look up at the huge sleigh drawn by reindeer; the apparatus was mounted on the highest roof of the mall. She could not hear it but she knew that loudspeakers were blaring out Christmas carols and other music that conveyed cheerfulness, family, friends, and fun.

Elena tried to pick up on the exuberance she knew was out there, some of it put-on and artificial, yet most of it sincere because who did not love Christmastime? Despite what she was taking in, however, she was in turmoil. Rafael's voice and face were stamped on her thoughts and she could not help feeling his burden, as if his loss were hers as well. She looked around at other drivers stranded in cars, some in conversation with a fellow passenger, others alone like her, and she wondered if any of them might be feeling a similar heaviness. She rubbed her eyes, trying to get a handle on the emotions that were flooding her but it was no use.

She was startled suddenly by irritated honking signaling that she had not moved her car forward, that there were a few empty feet in front of her car. She motioned her hand apologetically toward the rear window and stepped on the accelerator only to come to a stop again.

Certain thoughts loomed in Elena's mind. Rafael's family had been wiped out in a single night, but the more she thought about it the more she realized that it had happened in far less time; the calamity happened in a matter of minutes. That was all it took; a number of minutes counted on one hand and the whole family was wiped out. Although only three children perished under the gun leaving three members alive, these last three were lost as well. Elena took a hard look at that reality and figured that the father was hopelessly damaged, the mother would soon be executed, and Rafael? What about him? If his life did not straighten out, he might be close to extinction himself, or so she thought at that moment.

Elena focused on Rafael as his voice sounded vividly in her mind and she heard the anguished rage that had lashed out as he told his life story. She shook her head remembering what he said of his life as a child, his loneliness and terror, with no one to help him and she yearned to have been there to do something for him. But now the damage done to him was more than she could grasp. No matter how much she tried, she was incapable of even imagining what it might be like to experience the murder of one's siblings and, even more appalling, that their deaths were at the hands of his mother.

How many people suffer so much loss? Was the injury done to Rafael's spirit irreparable? Would he go on with his life a hopeless misfit? Her mind rejected this last question because the response might be too ugly, too repugnant. Instead she chose to think that he did stand a chance to live the life he wanted.

She looked beyond the hood of her car to see that the bottleneck was slowly loosening and that traffic had started to creep forward. She moved her car along with the flow while she looked toward the next light signal where she would make a right turn to her apartment.

Elena's thoughts shifted from Rafael to Rosario. She paused on the fact that despite what she had hoped in the beginning of her encounters with Rafael, questions regarding Rosario's crime had not cleared up for her. There was nothing in what she had researched nor in what Candelaria Fontes or Detective Haas said, that answered so many questions secretly hounding her. Did anyone actually see Rosario pull the trigger? Had her clothes been changed while she was unconscious? What about the weapon? Had it been tested? And what about her attorney and his obviously weak defense? Maybe the answers to these nagging doubts might indeed serve to confirm Rosario's guilt. On the other hand, they might prove her innocence. Whatever the case, until answered, these uncertainties lingered in Elena's mind leaving her unsure about Rosario's guilt or innocence. At the same time, however, she experienced a growing conviction that the resolution was out there waiting to be discovered. She again remembered Rafael's words spoken not an hour before saying that he was committed to pursuing the truth and now, for the first time, she felt that he could accomplish this mission.

She had not shared these thoughts with Rafael for fear of aggravating his nearly irrational belief in Rosario's innocence, but just thinking of it now agitated Elena so much that she lowered the window; she needed more air. In a few moments, however, she closed it when she felt rain drenching her arm and shoulder. Then she reached for the radio knob, hoping to get news or music, anything to distract her while she waited for traffic to clear up. Cheery carols chimed in and for once she found that jingle-jangle distressing, nerve-racking, so she punched to another station. More of the same jolly singing came through, so she shut it down and gave up on the radio.

So, what now, Elena? She leaned her head against the headrest, hearing herself pushing for an answer. She straightened her head and reviewed Rosario's words to Rafael, admitting to having bungled her life and allowing her children to drip through her fingers. What did that mean? How do children drip through a mother's fingers? The biggest challenge for Elena was Rosario's desire to end it all. Was that the wish of an innocent person, brave and unafraid because of a clear conscience? Or was it that death was the only escape from the intolerable desperation of guilt? Rosario said to Rafael that she wanted to be free, but free of what? Was it freedom from her caged existence or freedom from the anguish of guilt?

When Elena was preparing for her interviews with Rafael, she often pictured his mother's execution. In that scene she saw Rosario kicking and screaming dragged by guards to the death chamber. Her howling would be heard even by the crowd gathered outside the penitentiary, some in support, others in protest of her execution. However, that image had now changed in Elena's imagination. In this new vision, Rosario walked calmly to her death flanked by guards and chaplain. Soft murmurs and prayers filled the empty silence as she glided toward the chamber. Filled with this picture, Elena now pondered what kind of person approached execution that way: innocent or guilty? She did not know.

The only certainty was that Rosario Cota was going to be put to death and Elena asked herself why people found it necessary to execute someone in the name of justice. Was it to make up for a murdered life? Or was it to punish? Elena ran her hand through her hair knowing that no matter how much she tried, here was yet another answer she might never discover.

Up ahead rear-end brake lights were disappearing as vehicles lumbered forward. Elena straightened in her seat and shifted her foot from the brake pedal to the accelerator. She was finally moving and in a matter of minutes she turned down her street, then straight into the apartment complex where she parked.

Rain was falling hard but she made it to her place where she rushed into the small living room and switched on the lamp. She dropped her handbag and briefcase by the sofa, peeled off her coat, and kicked off her wet shoes. She took a minute to gaze out the front window to look at the neighborhood filled with Christmas lights and decorations. This reminded her that she had not put up a tree, a first time for her. She shrugged, reminding herself that she had been busier this year.

Elena ran her hands through her disheveled hair, shuffled to the kitchen, and opened the cupboard where she found the last of the scotch whiskey. She poured what was left into a glass, filled it with tap water, and then returned to the living room. She flopped into the easy chair where she sat thinking while she sipped the drink.

She had to admit that she was in turmoil, mostly because she was unsure of what to do next. When she began meeting with Rafael, she thought she knew exactly what was coming next, but now she was in a different frame of mind and she did not like the feeling. She knew that she needed to fix this restlessness so she let time pass while she listened to the rain, enjoying it because its rhythmic tapping began to relax her. After a time of reflection, Elena began to make a list of what steps to take next.

First on the list was her visit with Rafael on Christmas Day when she would try to make the day as enjoyable for him as possible. Then came planning the trip to New Mexico where she would meet Sister Gladys Miranda. After that came writing Rafael's story, putting on paper all that he had revealed to her. She knew that this task would be tough, nonetheless she would write the whole thing. The last step was the biggest challenge: assisting Rafael in the search leading to his mother's exoneration.

Elena's thoughts stopped abruptly. What was she thinking? Had she not doubted Rafael's plan to pursue his mission just a few hours before? Why was she now making his plan part of her future? She straightened up in the chair, thinking and questioning these changes in her but after a while she relaxed knowing that these uncertainties were useless, admitting that she had already made this decision long before; it happened while listening to Rafael. Even though doubts had crossed her mind several times, she no longer thought that he was a fool or a hopeless lunatic for wanting to reach this goal. Others had accomplished as much and so would he. It would take years, that was for sure, and it was bound to be a long uphill road but she made up her mind that she would walk that path alongside him.

Sketching out these steps calmed Elena. Feeling relieved and even optimistic, she drained what was left in the glass, switched off the lamp, and headed for the bedroom.

CHAPTER 23

Elena was right. Rafael was looking at her with unusual intensity as she left; he stared at the door long after she disappeared into the gloomy insides of the sanitarium. After a while he returned to the chair and dropped into it. The rain had started up again, coming with a chill that made him cross his legs and fold his arms closely over his chest. He was lost in thought as he watched the falling rain, its drops getting bigger and fatter, he thought.

Elena's voice echoed in his mind, making him feel lonelier now that she was gone. Her face lingered, its expression as moving and liquid as the rain splashing on the grass. He was thinking how her face had hardened when he spoke of renewing his intention to prove Rosario innocent and how it softened when she invited him on that trip to New Mexico.

Did she mean it? Would she trust him outside of Absalom House? He wanted to believe it but doubted that she would take the risk of being alone with him. Besides, he really did not want to go out there again. The thought frightened him. He rubbed his hands and then his face, telling himself that all that talk of going to New Mexico was just that: talk.

Rafael now felt a heaviness creeping up on him and he realized that his mouth was drying out; sourness began to coat his tongue. He swallowed gulps of saliva trying to dissolve the taste but it was no good because the bitterness only stuck more to the roof of his mouth. Trying to shake off the bad feeling, he reminded himself that he had felt good while Elena was with him just a short time before. Still, he felt himself slipping and no matter how much he tried, he just could not put his finger on why he was caving in to so much depression. But after a while he saw it. Whatever good feeling had been inside him began to fade when Elena questioned him about the dream.

This led him to thinking that now that his story was finished Elena would never return and then what would happen to him? Would he one day be smart enough to be on his own to prove Rosario's innocence? Would he ever live the good life he longed for? What about all the medication that was shoved down his throat everyday? Would the voices return without it to have a party inside his head? His ears buzzed as these questions jammed his brain and all the while the gloom inside him kept getting bigger, making him think more of the ugly pictures in the dream.

Trying to shake off the feelings that were assaulting him, Rafael got up from the chair intending to leave the room but instead he began to pace it. He did not know why he was walking; he just did it, crisscrossing the place, stomping from one corner to the other. He marched that pattern several times. Then he shifted what he was doing to shuffle parallel to the wall, kicking his legs up in the air higher and higher. As he did this he stretched out an arm and absentmindedly skimmed the wall with an outstretched finger, drawing an invisible line on the surface. He kept moving around the room faster and faster until he was panting from an exertion that finally forced his feet to drag clumsily.

He glanced out the window and saw that it was dark. Hours had passed since Elena left him but no one came looking for him so he stayed in the room. He kept up his nervous pacing while his mind whirled as if driven by gears and cogs, turning, looking, and searching, hoping to identify the shadow in the dream. He did this until his legs were drained of strength and he could go no farther. Then he headed for the chair where he had sat with Elena and dropped into the seat, lifted his knees, and wrapped his arms around them.

He put his face down between his knees and began rocking back and forth. He was thinking, trying to understand why he was so agitated and why he could no longer feel the way he felt before Elena left, but it was no use; he just did not know what was happening to him. He relaxed his legs and dropped his head on the back of the chair as he stared through the window at the black rain-soaked sky.

Rafael began to shiver and he tightened his arms around his chest, trying to shield himself from whatever it was that was making him tremble just like when he was a little boy. Now even his teeth were chattering and his chest was heaving as he tried to pump air into his lungs. Then he sat up, his body rigid because he suddenly realized what it was that was making him shake; he was afraid. He was terrified of so much, but mostly of Rosario and of her murderous rage. He was scared because he was a baby again, sitting in the crib waiting to be killed.

Rafael suddenly jerked to the edge of the chair and stared at the window with eyes wide open and pupils dilated. The dream that had knifed itself into his sleep ever since he could remember had now unexpectedly returned. There it was! Its images took shape and they were so vivid that they danced on the watery window in front of his eyes. The whole thing had suddenly crept out of its black hole while he was awake.

Rafael shook his head and rubbed his eyes trying to dispel what he was seeing but it was no use because the pictures would not go away. After a while the thought struck him that maybe it was not a dream; maybe it was something else. But if it was not a dream, what could it be?

He closed his eyes, hoping that when he looked again the images would be gone, but when his eyes snapped open it was all there. It took Rafael a long time to understand what was happening to him; his mind struggled, but then he knew. He realized that what he was seeing was not a dream after all but a memory buried inside him. What he had always thought to be a nightmare was really a recollection of what happened that night.

The memory recalled everything from the beginning of the killing rampage to the point where the shadow moved into his room. Now the form took shape, it did not vanish. It came close to him and looked at him as he sat in the crib. It was Rosario with a gun hanging from her hand. She looked at him for a long time and he knew that she wanted to kill him. Rafael sat frozen, staring at her, waiting for the bullet to smash his head, but it did not happen because it was a memory that went away as quickly as it had come. Suddenly it crept back into the crevice of his mind from where it had escaped.

Then everything stood still. The rain stopped its tapping on the window, his breath clung to his stiffened chest, even his thoughts froze. Rafael struggled as he rejected the memory, telling himself that it was impossible for him to remember what he had seen when he was a one-year-old kid. He was certain that what had just appeared to him was another fabrication of his mind, like the voices used to be. But Rosario's face hung like a mask in front of his eyes telling him that it was not the voices and that yes, he did remember.

A deep sadness invaded him, soaking into his veins, coursing through him like a toxic vaccine. Then he saw Abuela. It was just a glimpse because she, too, vanished out of sight as suddenly as she had appeared. But it did not matter to Rafael because he felt himself sinking into a pit so black that no one would ever find him. He was slipping into it fast and at the bottom of that abyss a monster weight was waiting to fall, ready to pound and crush him into nothingness. Soon he would be broken and nothing could ever put those pieces back into place. Words slipped out of his mouth.

"The bitch did it. She wasted the kids."

Yo! Ralphie Boy! You no-good piece of shit! You finally got it right. She did it and now you ain't got nowhere to run. Now what, asshole?

"Shut up! Goddamn you! Shut up! Shut up!"

Rafael's body jerked forward as he cried out and clamped his hands over his ears trying to drown out the voices that had unexpectedly returned from nowhere. He screamed over and again until his voice cracked, but there was nothing he could do about it. The voices had ambushed him, catching him utterly unprepared.

Ralphie, you know what you gotta do, right? It's all over, shithead. You know, oh, yeah, you know! So, what're you waiting for? Go on! Just do it, motherfucker!

The voices shoved him into the pit because they knew that for the first time in his life Rafael could not deny the ugly reality that was buried inside him. The unspeakable truth shattered him, slamming him back into the chair where his body stiffened even more, stretching out his legs grotesquely. His head slumped against the back of the chair; his mouth hung wide open. Whatever it was that had kept him alive to chase after the delusion of an innocent Rosario was sucking itself out of his body, leaving him empty and powerless.

Rafael remained that way for a long time; listening, eyes closed, limbs rigid, mouth gaping. No one saw him. He was alone. After a long while he snapped out of it, got to his feet, and shuffled to his room.

CHAPTER 24

Elena was in a deep sleep when the ring of the telephone yanked her out of it. Confused, she sat up, looked around; it was still dark, still raining. The phone rang for the fourth time and when her recorded voice kicked in her mind finally cleared. She glanced at the clock and saw that it was 3:30. She picked up and interrupted the nasal voice coming from the answering machine.

"Hello."

"Ms. Santos?"

"Yes. Who's this?"

"I'm calling from Absalom House. I'm sorry to call at this hour but you're the only one we know in contact with Rafael Cota."

"What's happened?"

"Can you come over now? It's better for you to be here."

"I'll be right over."

Elena jumped out of bed, threw on a sweat suit, slipped into running shoes and a raincoat, all the while trying to guess what trouble Rafael had caused this time. She knew that it was serious but that was as far as she allowed herself to guess. She ran out of her apartment, into the car, and soon she was sprinting up the front stairs of the sanitarium. When she rushed through the entrance, she found two interns waiting for her; their grim expression signaled bad news. One of them stepped toward her.

"What happened?"

"Ms. Santos, come over here, please. Let me get you a cup of coffee."

"No, thanks. Just tell me what's wrong."

"Rafael Cota killed himself."

"What?"

"He's dead."

Elena gaped at the intern while her brain tried to process his words, but no matter how much she struggled, her mind rejected what she was hearing. Trying to stall, her thoughts darted, latching on to unimportant details: a small ink stain on the cuff of the man's smock, his jaw covered with a beard that was barely a shadow. In those moments she knew that she resented him so much that she had to fight the impulse to slap him for telling her such a thing, in such a way. His bluntness horrified her.

"What are you saying?"

"He's dead."

"That's not possible! We were together just a few hours ago and he was fine."

"I'm sorry. Please let me show you where you can take a seat."

The intern took Elena by the elbow with the intention of helping her to a chair but she yanked away from him. Instead she glared at him while the reality of Rafael's death sank in and her mind accepted it. She looked at the man's face, finally understanding that what he was saying was not a lie, not his doing, and that it was real and irreversible.

"How?"

"He hung himself with a rope he made out of a bed-sheet."

"How can that be done in an open ward? That takes time. What about witnesses? Didn't anyone see what he was doing and try to stop him?"

"He was transferred to a private room some time ago. He was alone."

"Alone? Why?"

"Because he had improved so much. Surely you must have seen that yourself. We thought we had no reason to fear."

"Where's his doctor?"

Elena's voice was shrill, escalating, filled with tears. The intern kept silent. He did not attempt to defend himself or the staff; instead he listened to her respectfully, accepting her anger. When he spoke his voice was subdued.

"The doctor is out of town, but he's been notified and should arrive here by noon."

Elena became so faint that she was forced to take the chair the intern had given her. She closed her eyes trying to calm her racing heart; she felt her breath sticking in her throat and she was afraid of passing out. She took in large gulps of air, holding it in, then exhaling slowly and after a few minutes of breathing in and out she felt herself calming down. She looked at the intern and saw that he was offering her a glass of water. She took it and drank it down.

"I apologize. I'm very upset. He was my friend."

"We know, Ms. Santos. You're the only one he ever spoke of."

"He's got a father. He lives in Los Angeles."

"Yes. We tried that number but there's no answer. We've only reached a recording but we'll keep trying until we can speak to him."

"What about Sister Gladys Miranda? She lives somewhere in New Mexico."

"I couldn't locate that information. It'll have to wait until the doctor arrives."

"Why did you call me?"

"As I've said, you were important to him and we thought you should know."

Elena got to her feet still wobbly and she waited until she regained balance. All the while an idea was making its way into her mind, something that filled her with fear but it was something she had to do no matter how much her knees shook; no matter how much her heart pounded.

"Please take me to him."

"View the body? I don't know if that's a good idea."

"Take me to him!"

"Are you sure?"

"Yes!"

"He died by strangulation and even though we've been able to repair some of the damage, you should understand that his face shows that struggle."

"Repair? What do you mean?"

"Closed the eyelids. Put the tongue back in place. Readjusted the jaw."

"Oh, Jesus!"

"Yes. I advise against going in there."

"Take me to him. Please."

The intern looked at Elena for a few seconds, his face betraying concern as well as uncertainty; he was weighing what to do. He lowered his head and stared at his shoes, obviously struggling with the decision. In a few moments he looked up at Elena and nodded.

"Follow me."

Elena and the intern approached a hallway leading to wide swinging doors. There was no movement or action as they approached; they were the only ones heading for the room where she supposed Rafael's body had been placed. The corridor was dimly lit when they first turned into it, but as they moved sensors turned on powerful overhead lighting giving off illumination so brilliant that she blinked at the unexpected reflection.

The intern opened and held one of the doors waiting for Elena to step into the room, but when she entered she froze for a moment, surprised by the vastness of the place. Its walls were lined with stainless steel cabinets, tables, and sinks; instruments covered much of the counter space. She was struck by the antiseptic condition of the room. Spotless tiles covered the floor and the walls were painted stark white; the overhead neon lights transformed the intern's face into a white mask. Wheeled gurneys were placed neatly in the center, and after a few moments Elena saw that one of them held Rafael's body; an oversized sheet covered it.

"We're in the hospital wing. As you can see, we're equipped for pretty much any emergency that comes up. Except for suicide, that is. We're waiting for the coroner's office to come for Rafael's body."

"Why the coroner?"

"Suicide. Anything other than death by natural causes becomes coroner's business. It's the law."

"Until when?"

"What do you mean?"

"The coroner will keep Rafael until when?"

"Until the body is claimed by the next of kin."

"What happens if his father doesn't claim him?"

"We believe he will. After all, he's paid the bills for Rafael's treatment here at Absalom House. It's a hefty amount of money. He must care."

"Paying bills doesn't mean he'll come running."

"Ms. Santos, don't do this to yourself. It's too hurtful. You've been Rafael's friend and at this point I think it's best if you take all of this step by step. I'll be outside this door in case you need me. Take all the time you need."

The intern left Elena; the door swung back and forth on squeaky hinges before it came to a stop, leaving her in silence. She was terrified. She feared getting near Rafael, but she was even more frightened at the thought of removing the sheet from his face, because she had never been close to a dead body. She was so afraid that she wanted to run out of that colorless place and not stop until she fell off the cliffs that divided land from ocean. But she did not run; instead she forced her feet to take her to his side.

Shivering, she peeled down the sheet, exposing Rafael's face and shoulders. Seeing the heavy welts ringing his neck took the air out of her lungs and again she felt that she was going to faint, but she forced herself to stand steady. She looked at his face for a long time, at its distorted lips stenciled in purple, its eyelids swollen and bruised by strain. Her eyes followed the chiseled profile that had so often held her gaze, as well as the wide, strong cheekbones. Except for the purple tints blemishing his complexion, it still held the soft brown tones that had given his face so much beauty. Elena noticed a few strands of hair that had fallen on his forehead, so she gingerly swept them back into place, feeling the chill of his skin on her fingertips.

Every part of her was grieving, but she could not cry; a stiff knot in her throat blocked that sadness from finding an escape. She looked at Rafael Cota thinking that death had crept up on him silently, without warning, snatching him away before it did his mother. Now Rosario's four children were dead; whatever evil scheme had ordained this terrible tragedy was fulfilled.

Elena experienced the weight of responsibility bearing down on her as she thought of her part in what had come over Rafael. How could she have been so wrong in thinking that he had improved? What signs of distress had she missed? Convinced that she was too tired to listen, she had ignored his words uttered just a few hours before and she had walked away from him.

I don't know how my brain is gonna act up next. What I do know is that I don't want all this pain no more. Like Rosario, I wanna be free.

Elena listened to the echo of his voice, finally understanding that Rafael's soul was screaming out, telling her that he wanted to be free. But what she had not grasped at that moment was that it was in death that he would seek liberation. Yet he had sounded so firm in his plan to pursue Rosario's innocence, so much so that he convinced her, Elena, of its likelihood. Did this not affirm his desire to live? What went wrong between their last hour together and his final moments? She recalled the apprehension she had felt wondering how he would cope with Rosario's death, but she had been too much the coward to even utter that question. Was this the key? Was he escaping the horror of seeing his mother executed by taking his own life? At this point Elena's mind floundered; it could go no farther.

She tried to say something out loud just to let some of her feelings escape but her throat was choked up. Instead she gently pulled the sheet over Rafael's face, making sure it was covered and that the edges of the sheet were secure. She stared at the form for a long time not knowing what to do because her mind had gone blank and her heart seemed to have stopped beating. A while later she thought she heard the squeaky door open; when she turned she saw the intern waiting for her and she walked toward him.

"Are you all right?"

"Yes. I'm leaving."

They walked down the hallway toward the lobby of the sanitarium without saying anything. When the intern led Elena to the front exit she stopped for a moment.

"Will you let me know of anything new?"

"You mean his burial services?"

"Yes."

"Of course. Would you like me to have the doctor call you when he arrives?"

"Yes. Thanks."

Elena walked out of the sanitarium, heading for her car as she had done so many times before. It was still dark and the rain had stopped but she walked quickly as if to avoid getting wet. Once inside her car she slipped the key into the ignition, turned it, and listened to the soft purr of the engine. She put her hand on the gearshift but did nothing; instead she leaned her forehead on the upper rim of the steering wheel and cried.

She wept without restraint for the loss of Rafael. His mother's deeds had cheated him of a good life, making him believe that he did not belong; in the end he plunged head-long into unspeakable loneliness, compelling him to choose death over life. She also cried for what she, Elena, had done because she knew that when she came to him in the beginning it had been to meet him not as a person, a man, but only as a story, and she now felt ashamed and sorry. Later on she had changed but she did not let him know; she missed the chance to tell him she believed in him. She thought of their last hour together when she had wanted to embrace him and tell him that he could be loved and that he could be free. She had ignored that impulse and walked away from him. This more than anything grieved her, knowing that telling him might have made a difference. But there was nothing she could do now; the moment had come and gone.

Elena wiped her face, put the car in gear, and pulled out of her parking spot. When she rolled the car onto the street, it was still empty; only one or two cars cruised by. When she looked in the rearview mirror, she caught just a glimpse of the stairway leading up to Absalom House. She stepped on the gas and headed home to her apartment.

217

Day of the Moon

El Día de la Luna

En Busca de Bernabé

Erased Faces

The Memories of Ana Calderón

In Search of Bernabé

Song of the Hummingbird